George Bancroft

Martin Van Buren to the End of His Public Career

George Bancroft

Martin Van Buren to the End of His Public Career

ISBN/EAN: 9783337061517

Printed in Europe, USA, Canada, Australia, Japan

Cover: Foto ©Raphael Reischuk / pixelio.de

More available books at **www.hansebooks.com**

Martin Van Buren

TO THE END
OF HIS PUBLIC CAREER

BY

GEORGE BANCROFT

NEW YORK
HARPER & BROTHERS, FRANKLIN SQUARE
1889

PREFACE.

MANY years ago Silas Wright, then United States Senator from the State of New York, requested me to write a life of Martin Van Buren. I answered that I did not possess adequate materials for the undertaking. At a later day he brought me a singularly complete collection of manuscripts, including letters and papers extending to the end of Van Buren's public career. From these and other sources I prepared a concise record of the events of his life. The manuscript was seen by Van Buren, who pronounced it, as a record of facts relating to himself, authentic and true.

At the time of its preparation the public mind was grievously agitated by party divisions on public affairs and on public men; the manuscript was, therefore, put aside for publication in times more favorable to a fairness of judgment on the character and career of Van Buren. In my recent revision of the original manuscript I have made no change that could affect Van Buren's approval of it as thoroughly correct.

September 2, 1889.

CONTENTS.

CHAPTER I.

PAGE

EARLY LIFE OF MARTIN VAN BUREN: 1782–1812.. 1

CHAPTER II.

EIGHT YEARS IN THE LEGISLATURE OF NEW YORK:
1812–1820 21

CHAPTER III.

THE STATE OF NEW YORK IN CONVENTION: 1821 62

CHAPTER IV.

EIGHT YEARS IN THE SENATE OF THE UNITED
STATES: 1821–1829 110

CHAPTER V.

VAN BUREN AS SECRETARY OF STATE, AS MINIS-
TER, AND AS VICE-PRESIDENT: 1829–1837 158

CHAPTER VI.

VAN BUREN AS PRESIDENT OF THE UNITED
STATES: MARCH 4, 1837—MARCH 4, 1841 192

LIFE OF MARTIN VAN BUREN.

CHAPTER I.

EARLY LIFE OF MARTIN VAN BUREN: 1782–1812.

PUBLIC life in America opens the widest avenue for the promulgation of truth. The millions, through the statesmen of their choice, give utterance to their aspirations, and write the ripened results of their experience and reflection in the statute book of the country. No career is more honorable than that of the man who, alike in private life and in public station, consistently and earnestly cherishes the principles and promotes the measures which advance the culture and power of the people. Such services, in the State of New York,

I

have most frequently sprung from the homes of the smaller freeholders. The proprietors, whose manorial estates had enjoyed the right of representation, declared for American independence; and one of them, Robert R. Livingston, drafted the resolutions by which the American Congress proclaimed its adhesion to what Washington called "the modern" code of maritime law; but the principles of our Revolution would not have been safe in the custody of landlords alone; and, happily, by the side of their vast estates lay the more numerous small freeholds, on which the plough was in the hands of the owner.

At one of these freeholds in Kinderhook, on the fifth day of December, 1782, just as the American war for independence was drawing to a close, Martin Van Buren first saw the light. His mother, who lived to see her son on the sure path to distinction, was a woman of exemplary piety; his father was a descendant of one of the families which first emigrated from Holland to America. Owning the modest farm which he cultivated, neither debt nor rent-day troubled him. A patriot of the Revolution, he loved the soil which held the graves of his forefathers for several generations, and of which he had assisted to achieve the independence, and with hearty assent he embraced the principles on which that independence was made to rest.

In the seclusion of his native village, of which the fertile soil well rewarded labor, the boyhood of Van Buren passed away in work on his father's farm, and in study at the new academy in his native village. On all sides and in all things the active mind finds education, The country was ringing with the great principles of independence and freedom ; the Hudson that flowed by him passes among the most exciting scenes of the struggle for independence ; and the fresh traditions of the Revolution

trained his mind to the love of country
and the principles of civil freedom. From
earliest years he demanded reasons for
opinions, questioned authority, and sought
for general principles as the guides to convictions. Thus he grew up, without the
benefits and without the prejudices of tra-
ditional learning, depending on the ideas
and principles of American life as his
guides. Early habits of industry and self-
command formed themselves in the healthy
moral atmosphere of the farmer's household, under the eye of an affectionate father, and of a religious and devoted mother.
Much of his future celebrity may be traced
to the unpretending virtues which pervade
the families of our agricultural class, and
give to their sons natural dignity and self-
reliance.

The possession of the elective franchise
insures the political education of the people. Truth, though it may be not unmixed
with error, is diffused by rival parties, and

the questions that interest the civilized world are brought to the home of every citizen. He that has the elective franchise has influence on his own nation and in his degree on the destiny of humanity.

In the year 1796, at the age of fourteen, Van Buren, whose activity of mind gave his parents early hope of his success in life, began the study of law, still remaining under his father's roof. It was the period when America, having achieved its independence and adopted its constitution, was framing commercial connections with the civilized world. Everywhere jealousy was excited lest European intercourse should introduce the political maxims of the European policy of that day. The treaty with England, which divided the republic into parties, had been negotiated by John Jay, a citizen of New York; and from Robert R. Livingston of the same State it had encountered the severest strictures for its violation of the principles of maritime law.

Livingston, as he inveighed against the self-ish commercial code of England of that day, asked: "What is the law of nations? Is it not a rule of justice which reason prescribes as arising out of the existing state of civilized nations? Is not this varied as civilization improves? The law of nations among cannibals justifies eating their prisoners. Greeks, Romans, and Carthaginians condemned captives in war and their families to perpetual slavery. Will any one say this is still the law of nations? The principles of the armed neutrality are consonant with the rights of neutral nations, and any independent people may justify a war in their support."

The members of the Republican party of New York, at its first organization, blending liberal commercial principles with faith in the people, joined in the support of Thomas Jefferson, the Virginia civilian, for the Presidency. Their zeal so kindled the youthful mind of Van Buren that, in 1800, in his eighteenth year, the Republican party of his vicinity sent him as their delegate to a Republican convention of the counties of Columbia and Rensselaer.

Near the end of 1802, Van Buren, still a student of law, repaired to New York, and in that city a year of close application was devoted by him to legal studies. His powers were tested and developed by discussions in an association of young men, who, like himself, were preparing to be counsellors and advocates. At the close of 1803 he was admitted to the bar of the Supreme Court of the State of New York, and returned to his native village to engage in his profession. And now came the happy period of early activity and the rapid gain of distinction. Van Buren's ability and industry, his integrity and kindly frankness, rapidly won for him professional eminence, and led to friendships as enduring as life. Eight years flowed on in the serene happiness of domestic life and the increase of business, popularity, and fame.

His professional career called all his faculties into exercise, disciplined him in self-reliance, and laid the foundation of reciprocal confidence between himself and the great body of people of his own neighborhood. The soil of New York in the time of its colonial dependency, and under its royal governors, had been lavishly conveyed by royal patents, which squandered away hundreds of thousands of acres. These grants, which were usually made without a previous survey, and with no more definite boundaries than a reference to some uncertain brooks or hills, defined only by their Indian names, included large parts of Vermont and of Berkshire County in Massachusetts, as well as tracts on the water-shed of the Hudson, and from their imperfect description opened the way to incessant litigation. When Van Buren entered on his profession he found that some of the heirs of these indefinite patents, stimulated by the rapid increase of the population in that part of New York, applied the largest interpretation to their grants, and were then encroaching on a humble class of free-holders. The three distinguished lawyers of the vicinity, Abraham Van Vechten, Elisha Williams, and William Van Ness, were generally retained by the claimants under ancient warrants; the small freeholders looked to Van Buren, beseeching him to investigate their titles and defend their rights of possession. The tenantry, too, came to him to learn the nature and extent of the reciprocal obligations imposed by their leases. In defending their rights against encroachments, Van Buren stood alone, resisting analogies drawn from the English courts, and having the ablest of his seniors at the bar arrayed against him. By nature intrepid, he had the caution which is the rightful companion of courage. In his contests at the bar he relied on the clearness of his narrative and of his exposition of the law. Unskilled in appeals to passion, yet gifted with a rapid eloquence, he excelled in calmness and urbanity; and by the trust of the body of the people, the farmer's son of Kinderhook from very early life was borne onward in his professional career. Coming to encounter the best minds at the New York bar, he was roused by every generous incentive to make the efforts which gained him the respect and confidence of the soundest lawyers of his State. At a very early period of his life the desire grew up for his appointment to a high judicial station.

On his removal to Hudson in 1809, he continued to live in friendship with the people. When the defence of a cause required fearless regard for right, combined with superiority to influence, the popular opinion inclined to advise a resort to Van Buren. With equal frankness and resoluteness, Van Buren was interested in the rights

and honor of his country. Living in a federal county, with the avenue to public life
apparently barred against him, he stood in
the front rank of Republicanism, ready at
the polls, in conversation, at public meetings, in conventions, to assert the great
principles of maritime freedom and popular
rights. It was the period of long-continued
aggressions upon our commerce and our
mariners by Great Britain, who had assumed the dominion of the sea. America
gave to mankind an example of a renuncia-
tion of the benefits of foreign trade, rather
than to submit to the usurpation. American statesmen of that day had been actors
in the Revolution, and the embargo and
the system of non-intercourse were but
new forms of old measures of protection
and defence.

During this period Van Buren was foremost in Columbia County in the defence of
the principles which America was left almost alone among nations to keep alive.

His support of the administrations of Jefferson and of Madison was zealous, able, and persistent, and all the more weighty from the trust in his natural caution. In Columbia County, the Federalists seized the years of gloom to mislead the people; and, sustained by the influence of large landed proprietors over their tenants, they held public meetings to excite discontent and disturbance. On the instance of Van Buren, counter-meetings were immediately called; and at Hudson, in February, 1809, he led the unanimous resolves that " war, submission to European despots, or prohibition of commerce " were our only alternatives, and proclaimed it "the duty of every friend to the United States to come forward and express his determination to support the laws and constituted authorities of his country against every opponent, and to any extremity." A county meeting was summoned by a strong appeal from Van Buren, then chairman of the Republican committee in Hudson; and in that month, while Thomas Jefferson was President of the nation, he, with dignity and impressiveness, explained the wrongs inflicted on our country by the belligerent powers, defending the Government and its supporters against the calumny of being "enemies to commerce," urged that opposition to the administration which was the choice of the people would prove a dereliction of patriotic duty, and closed by offering, among others, the following resolutions:

"*Resolved,* As the sense of this meeting, that the decrees and orders of France and England are the real cause of the interruptions to our commerce and the consequent embarrassment of our citizens; and that our Government, by submitting to these decrees and orders, would have destroyed the independence and surrendered the sovereignty of the American nation.

"*Resolved,* That the members of this meeting, entertaining a high undiminished regard for the constituted authorities of our country, and warmly and fervently devoted to its honor and interests, do solemnly engage to support the Government in measures to

obtain redress for our national injuries, and protection to our national rights; that they never will be
driven from a fair and manly support of this resolution by the power of our enemies or the threats of
factions, and that, should Government be forced to
abandon the pacific policy it has pursued and un-
sheathe the sword, they will be found at their posts
ready and willing to sacrifice their lives and fortunes
in their country's cause."

In April, 1810, the Republicans of Hudson
came together to respond to the nomination
of Daniel D. Tompkins for Governor; and
Van Buren, as their chairman, renewed to
committees of other towns expressions of
indignation at " the flagrant violation of our
neutral rights." "We applaud"—such were
his words—"we applaud the wisdom and
the integrity which have been evinced by
the American Government in resisting and
repelling those violations. We observe on
our part an administration impelled to action by principles of the purest patriotism;
recognizing in their intercourse with other
nations the fundamental rules of national

justice; demanding nothing wrong, but firm in the maintainment of our rights. And we feel ourselves bound, by every tie which connects us to our country, publicly to express our unaltered determination to support the government of our choice, and at every hazard to stand or fall with our national independence."

The next year, at a similar meeting, Van Buren, by the general voice, was charged to draft resolutions; and on the evening of the 11th of April, 1811, he reported a series, of which the following is the first:

"*Resolved*, That we still entertain undiminished confidence in the integrity, wisdom, and patriotism of James Madison, President of the United States; that we have fully realized in his administration what we formerly anticipated before his election; and that he is eminently entitled to the esteem and veneration of every consistent Republican."

Other questions of moment mingled in New York with the great contest for maritime freedom. The first bank of the United

States drew near its end. A bill for the renewal of its charter passed the House of National Representatives and came to the Senate, where, on the 20th of February, 1811, it was rejected by the casting vote of George Clinton, a veteran of the War of the Revolution, once the Democratic Governor of New York and at that time the Vice-president of the United States. In this manner the question was specially brought home to the Democracy of Hudson River. This vote of George Clinton met with the hearty approbation of Van Buren.

The Democracy of New York had been resisting the intrusion of the moneyed influence into the public halls of his own State. The Bank of Manhattan was charged with obtaining its charter surreptitiously. A powerful association, on the certainty of the discontinuance of the United States Bank, strode boldly into the State Legislature, with petitions in one hand and bribes in the other; and by the offer of a bonus of four hundred thousand dollars and a loan to the State of two millions, attempted to extort a charter for a national bank of six millions. The establishment of this bank was opposed by some, because the moneyed interest intruded itself corruptly into the General Assembly; by others, for this reason, and further, because, in itself, the bank would form but a substitute for the Bank of the United States, and would exert the same baleful influence. For these considerations, the venerable George Clinton was opposed to it; and Van Buren, in private life a resident of a county where the so-called Federal party was in the ascendent, stepped forth to rally public opinion against corruption in its incipient stages. To a convention in Columbia County, which he had united in calling, he pledged himself against the recharter of the bank and against the system from which it sprung.

Yet, such was the influence of the applicants, such the systematic favor of a part

of the Legislature, such the force of corruption, that the Assembly, in the spring of
1812, manifested a readiness to grant the
proposed charter.

At this crisis, Daniel D. Tompkins, then
Governor of New York, resolute to secure
to the people an opportunity for its interposition, by an act of executive power that
was sanctioned by the old constitution, which
permitted a prorogation of the Legislature
by the Executive, but not the veto of enactments, prorogued the Legislature from
March 27th to May 21st.

This bold act threw the Federalists of
New York into a frenzy; and at this moment the Democracy of the district summoned the lawyer' who had been the frank
supporter of Jefferson and of Madison to
be their candidate for the Senate.

The visible approach of war, the defeat
of the Bank of the United States, and the
arrest of cupidity in the Legislature of New
York by its prorogation, inflamed party

spirit to its intensest fury. The interest of the election was concentrated in the middle senatorial district of the State, where Van Buren was the candidate. His comparative youth, his want of powerful family connections, the hostility of the seekers of privileges from the State Legislature, all conspired to raise up against him the most determined opposition. In one of the counties the Democratic vote was largely diminished by the united efforts of the manorial interests, of which the influence had formerly been divided. The news was brought rapidly of the defection in that county. The Federalists were sure of success. Their principal lawyers were descending the Hudson River in the same boat with Van Buren to attend the courts at New York, and could not suppress their exultations. Every moment brought news of the deep excitement that had pervaded the country. As the boat passed one of the towns on the river, a messenger came on board with a letter which announced the vote of Orange County. Van Buren was elected, though by a major-ity of less than two hundred out of more than thirty thousand votes; and, although that steamboat was freighted with the re-sults of the various elections throughout the State on which depended the Council of Appointment and the large patronage at its disposal, the first question that proceed-ed from the crowd that was waiting her arrival on the dock at New York was: How ended the senatorial election in the middle district?

So earnestly contested an election had hardly been known, as this by which Van Buren, while not yet thirty years old, was elected to the Senate of his native State for the period of four years from the 4th of July, 1812.

CHAPTER II.

EIGHT YEARS IN THE LEGISLATURE OF NEW YORK: 1812–1820.

ON the 18th of June, 1812, war against Great Britain was enacted by Congress. In the condition of the frontier of New York on the side of Canada, this transition from restrictive measures to the taking up of arms preceded adequate preparations for war. From boyhood Van Buren had held that the defence of mutual rights would justify a resort to arms, and war having "been declared," says William L. Stone, a political adversary, long a resident of Columbia County, "no public man in the State supported it more thoroughly, heartily, and zealously throughout than Van Buren." The Legislature to which he had been chosen was specially convened in November. Van Buren was the youngest man in the Senate, the youngest ever elected to that body. But the friends of the national administration, all who were resolved to sustain the war, with one voice accepted him as their leader. Not a week had he been in the Legislature, when in November, 1812, he proposed by an address to assure the Government that "the Senate will cheerfully and firmly unite their exertions with those of the other departments of the Government, to apply the energies of the State to a vigorous prosecution of the war until the necessity of its continuance shall be superseded by an honorable peace."

Then followed the vehement debate in which the young senator acquitted himself with superior ability, triumphantly sustained the address, and was himself deputed to lead the Democratic Senate in a body in pledging to the Democratic Governor its adhesion to the measures of President Madison.

At that extra session, Presidential Electors were to be chosen.   In January, 1812,
the Republican members of the Legislature of Virginia assembled in caucus, nominated Madison for President, and selected an electoral ticket of men who were
pledged to his support.   In March of the
same year, the Republican members of the
Legislature of Pennsylvania came together
and made a like decision; and these nomi-
nations were affirmed by the acts of Democratic members of Congress.   In May,
1812, six months before Van Buren's senatorial term began, the Republican members of the State Legislature of New York,
who, by the party usage of that time, were
held to act for the Democracy of the State,
assembled in like manner, and, at a very
full meeting, eighty-seven out of ninety-
seven being present, unanimously made a
nomination of De Witt Clinton.   A committee was immediately appointed to in-
form him of his nomination, which he

forthwith and unconditionally accepted. The members who made this selection were moved by admiration of his talents; by confidence in his most vehemently expressed opposition to the Federal party; by the feeling of State pride; by his popularity, derived in some degree from his friend and kinsman, the venerable George Clinton; and by the belief that the most efficient war President would be a citizen of the State whose commerce had been most injured and whose frontier was the most exposed.

The same Democratic senators who had united in this nomination of De Witt Clinton, the day after the declaration of war but before the news reached Albany, resolved that "the existing state of the country demanded an unequivocal expression of sentiment from every member of the Union; and that, under this impression, the Senate pledge themselves to support such measures as shall be adopted by the

General Government for the vindication
of our violated rights and honor." To a
man, they voted against an amendment
proposed by Judge Platt, a leading Federalist, and supported by the seven Federalists of the Senate, asserting that "neither the honor nor the interests of the
United States require that a war should
be declared against either of the belligerent nations of Europe; and that the system of non-intercourse and embargo, as
lately practised by the Government of the
United States, is hostile to the best interests of our country." A copy of the adopted resolution was sent to President Madison.

In the nomination of De Witt Clinton,
thus officially made, tendered, and accepted, Van Buren had no agency; but coming
into the Legislature which in November
was to choose electors, he united with majorities of Republican members of each
branch in the appointment of the regularly

nominated ticket of electors known to be in favor of Clinton. In the efforts of the friends of Clinton to advance his pretensions in other States, Van Buren took no share, nor were his relations with the Federal party for a moment changed from that of the uncompromising opposition, by which they had been before and were afterwards distinguished. He left no opening for doubt as to his purpose of supporting with his utmost ability the Democratic administration. At the meeting of the Legislature in 1813, the political relations between Van Buren and Clinton were dissolved and were never renewed; and Van Buren led the Democracy in its support of the war and of the measures of Madison.

The Senate had a majority of Republicans; the House had a still larger majority of Federalists; yet, never dispirited, Van Buren was eager to devise means for insuring success to the conduct of the war. It is the beauty of our federal system,

that in addition to the resources of the
General Government, each State has power
to minister to the public wants.   It was
resolved by the Democracy in these hours
of danger to bring the credit of the State
in aid of the credit of the Federal Government; and John Taylor, of Albany, offered
a resolve, directing the comptroller to subscribe four hundred thousand dollars to
the United States loan of sixteen millions.
Van Buren spoke in behalf of the measure,
and on the 12th of March it passed the
Senate by a vote of fifteen to eleven.   The
Assembly, which was controlled by the Federal party, would do nothing.

" The war," said Josiah Ogden Hoffman,
in the debate, " was unnecessarily and un-
justly commenced.   All the alleged causes
of the war, in comparison with the evils
necessarily arising from this unhappy contest, sink into utter insignificance."

" I," cried Elisha Williams, " will not furnish the administration with the means for

carrying on this war; I would starve them into peace with all my heart. The Government dare not impose taxes, because they are conscious that the war is unjust and unnecessary. They know, and we know, that the people will not bear taxes for such a cause."

Such was the temper of New York Federalism in the first year of the war. Against it the New York Democracy relied on the tongue and pen of Van Buren. An address from the Democracy of the Legislature to their constituents, every word of which was written by Van Buren, aimed at convincing every honest man "of the high justice and indispensable necessity of the attitude which our Government had taken, of the sacred duty of every real American to support it in that attitude, and of the parricidal views of those who refused to do so."

In glowing language he made a summary of the causes of the war; and of the prelimi-

nary efforts at redress by means of the embargo and non-intercourse ; he described the
British Orders in Council as "a direct attack
upon the sovereignty of the American people, to which a submission involved a surrender of independence." He recounted
the breach of faith on the part of England
in disavowing the treaty with Erskine for
the revocation of the Orders in Council.

"When the feelings of the American
people," he continued, "were at the highest
pitch of irritation in consequence of the
perfidious disavowal, a minister was sent,
not to extenuate the conduct of his prede-
cessor, but to fling contumely and reproach
in the face of the Executive of the American nation, in the presence of the American people. . . .

"To fill up the measure of our wrong,
she resolved to persist in another measure,
surpassed by none in flagrant enormity—
a measure which, of itself, was adequate
cause of war; a measure which had excited

the liveliest solicitude and received the
unremitted attention of every administration of our government from the time of
Washington to the present day—the wick-
ed, the odious, the detestable practice of
impressing American seamen into her ships
of war; compelling them to waste their lives
and spill their blood in the service of a foreign government ; a practice which subjected every brave American tar to the violence
and petty tyranny of a British midshipman,
and many of them to a life of the most gall-
ing servitude; a practice which never can
be submitted to by a nation professing a
claim to freedom; which never can be ac-
quiesced in by Government without rescinding the great article of our safety—the reciprocity of obedience and protection. . . .

" Under such accumulated circumstances
of insult and injury, we ask again, What
was your Government to do? Was she
basely and ingloriously to abandon the
rights for which you and your fathers had

fought and bled? Was she so early to
cower to the nation who had sought to
strangle us in our infancy, and who has
never ceased to retard our approach to
manhood? No; we will not for a moment
doubt that every man who is in truth and
fact an American will say that war was our
only refuge from national degradation, our
only course to prosperity."

In the midst of these scenes, the Assembly yielded to the subtle influence of men
eager to grow rich by the use of credit,
and not sufficiently considering that coin
is money, and paper is only the promise
of money, prepared to go largely into the
chartering of banks of emission. They
would have no war for maritime rights;
but they were ready to risk the establishment of American industry and trade on a
paper currency.

When, early in 1813, a bill was brought
into the Senate to charter the Bank of On-
tario, Van Buren, in this first winter of his

legislative career, moved that the bill be rejected, and his motion received thirteen votes against thirteen; so that the bill would have been defeated but for the casting vote of the chairman.

Immediately a new effort was made to charter the Catskill Bank. Again, without the full adhesion of his party, Van Buren moved the rejection of the bill, and supported the motion by an elaborate argument.

"It is," said he, "but the creation of a fictitious capital, the substitution of a representative of money for money itself. From the very nature of the business, it is subject to danger; and the fictitious character of the capital subjects the realities of the country to an irresponsible fund.

"Confidence can alone be sustained by the belief that it is, what it purports to be, a representative of specie, and redeemable as such; and by the reliance on the virtue and integrity of the agents who emit it.

The destruction of either of these sources of confidence takes away the value of the paper; and our actual situation and the extension of banks must destroy both.

"Such is the proportion between the specie in the Union and the paper authorized to be issued, the belief in the ability of banks to redeem their paper, should any cause drive it to its source, is already, and must be, abandoned. The very manner in which our banks go into operation, on what is called foreign paper, shows that the idea of redemption by specie is not even indulged in at their very inception.

"Equally certain is the want of confidence in the agents. At the commencement of banking business, it was confined to men of high notions of credit; confidence must of necessity be destroyed by throwing the management of it, with chartered privileges, into the hands of everybody.

"Meantime, what is the situation of the

3

State? First, specie is driven out of circulation; next, trade becomes extensive in the proportion in which the amount of supposed cash has been extended. But the value of everything bears a proportion to the value of your money. The good-sense of the community must ultimately impair confidence in bank paper; the failure of a single bank would consummate it. And when paper-money is all the money we can depend upon to answer the purposes of trade, a depreciation in its value not only produces a like depreciation in the value of property, but an entire stagnation in business.

"Against only the sources of danger thus far delineated, what are the inducements to continue the accumulation of banks? Can any one doubt but that the increase of banks must, some time or other, lead to their destruction? Can any one say or expect that there will be a more fit opportunity to stop than now?"

He then recapitulated the history of the
New York banks from the first Bank of
New York; he did not omit one; and he
analyzed the influence of each under the
false system of privilege in hastening their
general bankruptcy. He dwelt on the danger that was joined with the qualified benefits which merchants derived from them;
he drew "a contrast between the merchants
of this day and of former times, when there
were no banks"; he showed the relation of
"farmers" to banks, and gave "the reasons
why bank accommodations are to them the
deadliest usury."

Passing from general consideration, he
dwelt on the imminent danger resulting
from the manner in which banks were conducted, and the nature of their loans; he
appealed to patriotism, and drew arguments
for a sound currency from the existence of
"the war"; he dwelt on the extreme "solicitude of the public," and justified that
solicitude.

Finally, he met the argument of those who looked for the safety of the public in the supervising power of the State Government. "What," he exclaimed, "the banks under the control of the Legislature! The mistaken idea!" And he pointed out at least four several instances, fresh in the knowledge of his hearers, where the Legislature, far from exercising control, had bowed its neck to the most subtle of external influences.

These views on banking, its abuses and its dangers, were expressed by Van Buren in the first year of his public life. The majority of that day was deaf to his appeals; but he never ceased to renew them. At the same session, on the question of chartering the Bank of Lansingburg, Van Buren seconded the motion for the ayes and noes, and voted against the bill throughout all its stages. He combated the bill for the Bank of Orange County in every stage of the proceedings, and obtained the rejection of its first section ; but the bank party rallied, and reconsidered the vote. Still he persisted ; and the charter for a bank at Schenectady was rejected on his motion.

Meantime, a new form of corruption required to be resisted. The City Bank of New York had obtained a charter at a previous session ; it now solicited relief from an onerous condition, and a bill was reported for that purpose. At once Van Buren moved and urged its rejection. The Bank of America came into the Legislature with a similar request. For that, too, a bill was reported ; and Van Buren exerted every nerve to effect its defeat, pursued the subject from day to day, thrice demanded the ayes and noes, and continued his determined resistance to the last. And when, in the same session of 1813, the Bank of Columbia asked authority to establish a branch at Athens, Van Buren moved the rejection of the bill.

But not all the efforts requisite to rouse the people to the support of the war, and to expose the insidious inroads of evil influences in legislation, could prevent Van Buren from thinking of private misfortune. As a senator, he was a member of the Court of Errors, and took part in the judicial interpretation of the laws. The application of an act for the relief of debtors had, by the lower court, been confined within the narrowest range. Van Buren contended that a merciful law should have mercy for its interpreter. " This statute," he urged in March, 1813, " has been passed for humane purposes; it was among the first concessions which were made by the inflexible spirit, which has hitherto maintained its hold upon society, authorizing imprisonment for debt. Coeval with the authority of imprisonment for debt have been the exertions of men of intelligence, reflection, and philanthropy to mitigate its rigor." And now the young senator gave

pledges for his future action by stigmatiz-
ing the practice as ruthlessly criminal and
" fundamentally wrong."

Van Buren, in his first legislative year,
sustained the war, foreshadowed the evils
of privileged banking, and protested against
imprisonment for debt.

The fervid appeal from his pen to the
people of New York was not made in vain.
In April, 1813, Tompkins, the supporter of
the war and of Madison, was elected governor by a majority of three thousand five
hundred votes. The Federalists still retained a majority, though a diminished one,
in the Assembly. The State of New York,
more exposed than any other, with a patriotic Senate and a governor not shunning
responsibility, was still arrested in its efforts at energetic self-defence by the negative of the Assembly; and the legislative
session of 1813–14 passed away with inef-
fective struggles for the vigorous conduct
of the war. Sometimes public conferences

were adopted as an expedient of conciliation.   At these, Van Buren appeared as
the principal speaker on the part of the
Senate.   Reasoning accurately, ever self-
possessed, having his mind kindled but not
disturbed by a just indignation, his words
fell upon enthusiastic auditories that came
in crowds to the Capitol.   On one occasion, the great audience was so moved that
at the close of his speech the venerable
Judge Hager, Senator from Schoharie, who,
himself a patriot of the Revolution, bore
with him the living recollection of the
ravages with which the British and the
Tories had scourged that section of the
State, was so thrilled with a speech of Van
Buren as to step forward from his place at
the moment of its conclusion and embrace
and salute him in the presence of the multitude.

   But Van Buren did not rest satisfied
with addresses to a stubborn opposition.
Baffled as yet in the Legislature, he ap-

pealed to the people. At his instance, near the close of the regular session of 1814, in the moment of gloomiest forebodings, a public meeting was convened at Albany, consisting of the Democratic members of the Legislature and citizens from various parts of the State. This general meeting was held on the 14th of April, 1814, and addressed by him at length and with great effect. He then submitted a series of comprehensive resolutions, which were adopted with enthusiasm. His hopefulness and un- questioning reliance on the people inspired confidence, and from that meeting there went forth an appeal to which the citizens of the State responded. In the midst of defeats in the field, New York rose up ra- diant with trust in its own energies, and gave a total overthrow to "the anti-Ameri- can spirit" which had so long enervated its power of decision.

This result was hailed everywhere by the friends of the Union, as "the triumph of

principle," with an exultation and joy scarce-
ly inferior to that with which the news of
the victory of New Orleans was received at
Washington. The war had triumphed in
the national opinion, which became the sure
presage of victories in the field. "The
election in the great and powerful State of
New York," said the *National Intelligencer*
of May 5, 1814, "resulting in the complete
success of the Republican party, has at once
overthrown the prospects of disorganizers
and the hopes of the Opposition. New York
is with the Government, and its colossal
power and influence will give vigor to its
operation by coincidences of action, instead
of lending its aid, as the Jacobins of the
East vainly hoped and predicted it would,
in a moral and physical effort to stop the
wheels of government. . . . If our enemies
please it, we shall have an honorable peace,
an event we should greet with heart-felt
pleasure; but if they persist in their wrongs,
the result of the New York election proves

that the people will support the Government in a vigorous war."

Van Buren, on entering the Legislature, took the lead in support of the war, and pursued it earnestly through two almost fruitless sessions; had for two successive years led the way in appeals to the people; and now he stood before the country the most conspicuous member of a Legislature in which his friends were a majority. Would he display intrepidity in council and vigor as a man of action?

The city of Washington had been seized, but from Baltimore the enemy had been repelled with grievous loss; the Niagara frontier had witnessed brilliant actions; on Lake Champlain, McDonough had won the highest honors for the American flag; while a small body of regulars, and an inconsiderable gathering of volunteers and militia of Vermont and New York, acting under an exigency which "admitted of no delay," discomfited the British land troops at

Plattsburg, and drove them to a precipitate flight.

An extra session of the Legislature was convened by Governor Tompkins on the twenty-seventh day of September, 1814. To his eloquent address Van Buren replied on behalf of the Senate in most impressive words, at a time when every act was of momentous interest. Immediately, by a message on the last day of September, the Legislature was invited to proceed to active preparations.

The Federal members of the Legislature of New York had issued a circular calling the Federalists of that State to a convention, which was held at Albany on the fifth day of October. There the propriety of sending members to the proposed convention at Hartford was considered, and rejected with unanimity. This decision appalled the disaffected. Meanwhile, Van Buren proposed, matured, brought forward, and carried through, what Thomas H. Benton has

described as "the most energetic war measure ever adopted in this country." It authorized the Governor to raise an army of
twelve thousand men for two years, and to
place them at the disposal of the General
Government. In raising this army, the system of an equal classification, acting on
property as well as on persons, was to be
followed; the men were to be paid, clothed,
and subsisted by the United States, and
were intended as a more permanent force
to relieve the militia. By this means the
undoubted superiority in the field was assured to America; and New York, which,
by its Legislature, in a resolution which
Van Buren introduced, advised the rejection of the arrogant British proposals for
peace, and prepared to have in service an
army of twenty thousand men.

The measure met with determined opposition. For two days the Senate of New
York debated whether troops should be
raised by voluntary enlistments, or by clas-

sification. On the twelfth day of October, the principle of classification prevailed by a vote of twenty to eight. On the 14th the bill passed the Senate; and having received the sanction of the Assembly, on the 24th, just five days after Massachusetts elected delegates to the Hartford Convention, Van Buren's bill, "authorizing the raising of troops for the defence of the State," received the signature of the Governor. The original draft, in the handwriting of its author, may be seen among the archives of the Senate.

This measure, after becoming the law of New York, was still the subject of discussion; and in the public journals the patriotic Samuel Young came forth to its defence on principles of public law. Voices from various parts of the Union approved it as worthy "of the best times of the Revolution, and as having exalted New York to the first rank in patriotism."

By degrees America learned the wealth

of her own resources; the news from Lake
Champlain and from Albany quickened negotiations; England receded from its ab-
surd demands, and a treaty of peace was negotiated. Yet the news of the negotiation
did not reach America until after the glorious repulse of the enemy from the country
had been perfected at New Orleans. It
then fell to the lot of Van Buren to suggest
to the Legislature of his own State those
" rewards of public service which are ever
due to the brave, the virtuous, and the wise";
and to draft resolutions expressing the applause and gratitude of New York for the ·
successful heroism of Andrew Jackson. Little was it then foreseen that these two men
as statesmen would be connected in the
closest bonds of friendship, founded on
common convictions, generous courage, and
success in the administration of public affairs.

The messenger bringing from Europe
the news of peace, found Van Buren in the

committee-room engaged in devising amendments to his bill for the classification of all
persons liable to military service, with a
view to the more easy and certain execution
of the law. In the financial embarrassment
of the country, the militia called into the
public service were without pay; Van Buren
recommended a loan by the State to the
General Government for the prompt payment of "the brave men who met and successfully resisted the veterans of the enemy
on the banks of the Saranac; to those who
performed tedious services at Sackett's Har-
bor, and on the western frontier; to that distinguished band who, under the gallant Por-
ter, stamped an indelible record of American
valor on the shores of the Niagara."

"The war," wrote Van Buren for the Senate in 1816, one year after its close, "was
not only righteous in its origin and successful in its prosecution, but our country
has arisen from the contest with renovated
strength and increased glory. To the na-

tion the elevation of our national character is wealth, strength, and the source of
happiness; confidence in the efficiency and
stability of our political institutions is the
sheet-anchor of their hopes, and the palla-
dium of their liberties." This is the part
which Van Buren took in the great war of
America for maritime freedom and equality
among the nations, or, as Edward Everett
named it, " our second war for independence."

In February, 1815, Van Buren, with universal approbation, was appointed Attorney-
general of the State. This advancement
led to his removal to Albany; but the people still retained him in the Senate.

The war had involved the national finances in embarrassment. Among the resolutions of the House of Representatives at
Washington, in 1814, was one declaring it
".expedient to charter a Bank of the United
States, with branches in every State." But
though the season of trial had come, when

4

with great reluctance, yielding to what seemed a necessity, wise and patriotic statesmen indulged the delusive hope of improving the national finances by the charter of a bank, Van Buren, still a member of the State Legislature, inflexibly resisted the concession.

In the Legislature of 1814 the bill to confer banking powers on the New York Coal Company was opposed by him, and rejected. The Wool Deposit and Wool Stapling Bank shared the same ambitions and met the same fate. The Assembly had chartered the North American Coal Company with banking powers; the clause conferring these powers was stricken out in the Senate; a conference ensued between the two houses, with Van Buren as chairman on behalf of the Senate, and on his motion the Senate adhered to its amendment.

The bill from the Assembly to establish the Dutchess County Bank was rejected in

the Senate, Van Buren voting against it,
and seconding the demand for the ayes
and nays.

At the extra session of 1814 Van Buren
persevered in his resistance, and his vote.
stands recorded against the Bank of Ge-
neva, the Bank of Plattsburg, the Bank of
Albany.

In 1816 the Jefferson County Bank met
with his opposition.

In 1818 the Cherry Valley Bank was rejected in committee, Van Buren being in the
chair and giving the casting vote against
it. The same opposition was made by him
to the branch of the Bank of Orange at
Binghamton, to the Catskill Aqueduct
Association, to the Utica Insurance Company, to the Franklin Bank, to the New
York Interest Bank, tŏ the North American Coal Company, and to the Greenwich
Bank; and in 1819 to the Exchange Bank.
He that will turn to the records of the
New York Senate will find Van Buren op-

posing steadily the whole system of banking of that day, giving his vote and using
his voice against at least thirty bills for
bank charters; and only in the single instance when the homeless inhabitants of
Buffalo, pointing to the ashes of their town
that had been burned by the enemy, declared that, desperate as might be the remedy, they must employ credit to rebuild it,
he omitted to oppose the prayer of misfortune, though he would never yield to the
importunities of avarice.   But in that one
exception to his uniform opposition, he
gave a warning that the hope of benefit
would prove delusive.

Nor did Van Buren content himself with
warning against the system in detail.   He
attacked it in its stronghold.   He saw the
great evil and temptation that lay in the
character of monopoly.   Finding it impossible to arrest this spirit of legislation as
long as the restraining law which prohibited unincorporated banking was in force,

he, as early as 1817, struck a blow at the principle of privilege, and introduced a bill to repeal that statute, and to authorize unincorporated associations to carry on the business of banking under the regulation of general laws. The bill contained the provision of individual liability, and also a provision to punish frauds in the conduct of banks by the ignominy of the penitentiary. After repeated efforts, the persistency of Van Buren won for his measure a majority in the Senate; it was lost in the Assembly.

This was the preparatory career, on the subject of banks, of the statesman who, on his participating in the Federal Government at the hottest moment of the controversy, avowed most publicly " uncompromising hostility to a Bank of the United States."

Van Buren was, from the commencement of his legislative career, active in his efforts to do away with the unnatural lien which, under the old laws, the creditor possessed on the body of his debtor.

As early as April, 1813, he introduced into the New York Senate, on leave, "A Bill for the Relief of Small Debtors." The journals of the same body show that during the sessions of 1817, 1818, and 1820 he was actively engaged upon the subject of imprisonment for debt, and that in 1818 he reported the "Bill to Abolish Imprisonment for Debt, and to Punish Frauds," and carried it through the Senate by the strong vote of twenty-one to five.

Nor was Van Buren unmindful of the great interests of his State in the development of its internal resources. The Erie and Champlain canals, from their novelty and grandeur of design, excited the admiration of the country, and seemed like dreams of marvel. Should New York, it was asked by the timid, attempt the anticipation of a century, and at an incalculable expense plunge into what might prove an impracticable adventure?

The project was moving forward under

the particular auspices of De Witt Clinton, between whom and Van Buren there existed at the time the most decided political antagonism. Moreover, many of Van Buren's warmest friends in various parts of the State, honestly doubting the success of the undertaking, and many believing that, even if successful, their part of the country would suffer by it, had arrayed themselves in opposition to the measure. None of these considerations affected his resolute mind. Having in 1813, in the first year of his senatorial term, voted against the repeal of the act further to provide for the internal navigation of the State, by which a board of commissioners had been established to prepare the way for this magnificent enterprise by examinations and surveys, he, from the beginning to the end of his senatorial career, gave to its accomplishment an unvarying and most efficient support.

During the winter of 1816 the commis-

sioners made a report to the Legislature.
Their labors had been interrupted by the
war; their surveys were as yet incomplete,
their estimates inexact, and in their report
they did not recommend "preliminary measures." Near the close of the session, a bill
for the immediate commencement of a portion of the work passed the House, though
a strong friend to the canal had moved to
wait for more exact surveys and estimates.
On the sixteenth day of April, but two days
before the adjournment, the bill reached the
Senate for debate. There was danger of
the total loss of the measure. Van Buren
stepped forward to save it by postponing
the immediate commencement of the work,
and confining the bill to obtaining more accurate surveys and estimates. The Legislature did not, as yet, possess such information as would avert the charge of hasty and
inconsiderate legislation.

In April of the following year, after the
mature exercise of the public judgment, a

bill for beginning the great enterprise passed
the House. The Senate seemed hostile to
the measure. It was then, when the decision was wavering—nay, when it seemed certainly adverse—that Van Buren rose to defend the bill. He reviewed the preparatory
measures of the State; he dwelt on the
more accurate calculations which were now
before the Legislature. "We are arrived,"
said he, "at the point where, if this bill does
not pass, the project must for many years
be abandoned;" and he pleaded for com-
mencing the work at once, from motives
relating alike to "the honor and to the interest of the State." With a just sentiment
of pride and regard to the Constitution, he
observed, " In no part of the business have
we looked to individual States, or to the
United States, for assistance." He pointed
out the means for meeting the vast expenditure, being unwilling to incur debt without
indisputably adequate resources.

"The vote I am to give," he added, " I

esteem the most important vote I have ever given in my life. The project, if executed, will raise the State to the highest possible condition of fame and grandeur."

"His speech"—so writes William L. Stone, a political adversary then present—" his speech was indeed a masterly effort. I took notes, but his manner was on that occasion too interesting to allow a reporter to keep his eyes upon his paper." When Van Buren resumed his seat, De Witt Clinton, who had been an attentive listener, breaking through the reserve which political collisions had created, approached him, and in terms the most honoring joined the general voice of admiration.

Long afterwards that eventful day was remembered; and Hosack, in his memoir of Clinton, pays a just tribute to Van Buren and his friends, as having " signalized themselves by rescuing the bill from a state of jeopardy, even when it had been to a certain degree abandoned by its friends." " By their personal and," he adds, "almost miraculous exertions, it was resuscitated, and again restored to the approbation of the two Houses of the Legislature."

But not only did Van Buren save the measure from defeat—he made it feasible. The bill, as it passed in the Assembly, authorized loans on the security of the canal fund only, and that was the best form in which, in the first instance, it could be carried through that body. The vital importance of extending the security was at the time fully appreciated, and soon demonstrated by experience. It was on the motion of Van Buren that the State pledged its faith for the repayment of the loans necessary to the construction of the canals.

Once more a crisis occurred in the progress of this grand enterprise. In 1819 there were not wanting timid politicians who desired to arrest the canal at the Seneca River on the one side, and midway in the Mohawk River on the other. Van Bu-

ren resisted both these impairments of the
great design, and the clause for construct-
ing the canal from Seneca River to Buffalo
was at last, through his unwearied exertions,
retained in the bill, though by the small majority of four.

Nothing better illustrates Van Buren's
character than his conduct on these occasions. For a wise project he was the daring
and unwearied advocate, steadfastly sustaining it in its proper proportions and grandeur. And all the while De Witt Clinton
was reaping the fruits of the measure which
Van Buren rescued, and, by means of popularity growing out of the success of the
canals, attained the highest station which it
was in the power of the State to confer.

Such was Van Buren, in the service of
New York, as a senator and as its chief law
officer. "He is a very eloquent speaker"—
this is the testimony of an able opponent;
—"his manner is graceful and animated
when occasion requires, or impassioned

when engaged upon an inspiring theme.
He has a happy command of language, but
his utterance is too rapid. With manners af-
fable and insinuating, he inspires his friends
with the strongest attachment known to political ties; and, though self-educated, his
professional knowledge is such as to have
placed him in the front rank at the bar."

CHAPTER III.

THE STATE OF NEW YORK IN CONVENTION: 1821.

At this time Van Buren was become the acknowledged leader of the Democratic party of New York. They had trust in his fidelity to principle and his wisdom in conduct. Through their confidence, a wider sphere of action was opening before him. But one great duty remained to be performed at home.

The fathers of our country, as they instituted popular government, had not as yet the lights of experience as guides. In New York, "a germ of aristocracy had mingled with the seeds of liberty which they planted; and it began to produce bitter fruit." By the constitutional charter, formed in 1777, all but freeholders and actual tenants were disfranchised, and the freeholders themselves were divided into two classes. Those of twenty pounds, New York currency—that is, of fifty dollars— could vote for representatives to the Assembly; but to vote for governor or senators required the possession of an unencumbered freehold of the value of one hundred pounds; that is, of two hundred and fifty dollars.

Van Buren, with his friends, proposed nothing less than to transfer the sovereignty of New York from the freeholders to the inhabitants of the State. "It was one of Van Buren's maxims," writes Hammond, in relation to this subject, "that that which ought to be done should be done quickly." And Van Buren himself, on another occasion, expressed his rule of conduct in these words: "Whatever is determined to be done, should be done at once. Deliberation, if it supply the place of action, is not less fatal than precipitation. To hesi-

tate and permit occasions to pass away
which can never be recalled, partakes of
the character of weakness, and detracts
from the reputation of any man, whether
in the Cabinet or in the field." In November, 1820, a special session of the New
York Legislature was convened. Both
branches were Democratic ; the flow of
popular opinion was for the government
of all by all. At once a bill was matured,
and passed the two branches of the Legislature, for calling together an unrestricted
convention of the people. The Council of
Revision was divided, and Governor Clinton, to universal surprise, negatived the
bill. At the regular session in the following January the question was reviewed
under the swelling impulse of a decided
popular will, and a law was enacted requiring that the question of calling a constituent convention should, at the election
of April, 1821, be laid before the people
for their decision. If the people concurred

with the Legislature, delegates to a constituent convention should be elected in June of that year, and the meeting of the convention should take place in the following August.

At the polls in April the people, with great unanimity, proclaimed their desire for a convention, to which the members should be elected by a greatly enlarged constituency.

In June, the men charged to lay anew the political edifice of New York were chosen. The county of Albany, in which Van Buren then resided, was of the so-called Federal party, and elected his political opponents, Kent, Spencer, Van Rensselaer, and Van Vechten. But the Democracy of Otsego County, as they afterwards affirmed with pride and gratitude, confiding in his fidelity to principle, without any previous communication, direct or indirect, selected Martin Van Buren, though a resident of another and remote county, and

5

personally unknown to them, to represent them in the convention.

On the twenty-eighth day of August the great assembly came together, charged to decide for New York, with the consent of the people, the persons who were to participate in the sovereignty and how it should be exercised. The talent assembled in the convention corresponded with the importance of the problems which it was to solve. There were Kent, then Chancellor of the State, Spencer, the Chief-justice, and Van Ness and Platt, Associate Justices of the Supreme Court, with General Van Rensselaer, Abraham Van Vechten, Elisha Williams, and others, commissioned to impede the onward movement to a government of all men by all men. There, too, were sent by the Republican party, Van Buren, Tompkins, Samuel Young, and many others of like vigor; and some who in later times fainted by the way. Tompkins being elected president, the topics for consideration were at once assigned to appropriate committees.

The chief purpose of the convention was the reformation of the franchise, to which Van Buren had already directed public attention. Presiding at a festival in Albany, on the fourth day of July, 1821, he had given as the leading sentiment for the day, " The elective franchise: Existing restrictions have proved to be as impolitic as they are unjust; it is the office of wisdom to correct what experience condemns." But it behooved him to move warily. The State of New York had for many years oscillated between the two great parties. At that moment the Democratic party was in the ascendent, and Van Buren saw himself in the convention surrounded by a great majority of his friends; but still the political character of the majority of the people was uncertain. From the first moment of the assembling of the convention his mind was full of solicitude for the result. " If," said

he, "we would effect those wise and salutary amendments which the public voice
and the public interest demand, we should
beware of vibrating to extremes." This was
his counsel given in the first great debate,
and adhered to throughout the session. On
various occasions he directed attention to
the feuds and bitter controversies which
would inevitably grow out of the loss of the
amendments to be adopted by the convention.

The first earnest discussion related to the
veto power which the New York Constitution of 1777 conferred on the majority in a
council of revision, composed of the Governor, the Chancellor, and the Judges of the
Supreme Court. Thus the veto resided essentially in the permanent judiciary, who
were irresponsible to the people for its use.
That there should exist a veto power on the
Legislature is the true theory of government by the people, which makes the executive dependent on the people for its exist-

ence and its continuance, and in its own
behalf intrusts to that executive a tribunitial power to arrest acts of legislation that
spring from precipitancy, corruption, or ill
judgment. The veto, thus conferred, can
but bring its appeal solemnly before the tribunal of the whole people, presenting for its
decision a question between the Legislature
which may represent a combination of local
interests, and the executive which repre-
sents the whole.

In the course of an argument marked by
manliness and good-sense Van Buren justly
observes: "Legislative bodies are subject
to passions, and sometimes to improper influence. Their acts are frequently so detri-
mental to the public interest that the united
voice of the people calls for their repeal;"
hence "the necessity of a controlling power.
What is the consequence of requiring two-
thirds of the Legislature to pass a bill which
may have been returned? It may prevent
the passage of a bad law, but never can de-

feat a good one.   If a good law be returned
with objections, it will at the next election
come before the people; they will pronounce
upon it, and return a representative who will
insist upon its passage.   If it be a bad one,
the revising power will be justified.   An instance of the abuse of power, thus confided,
has never existed where it did not defeat
the very object for which it was abused. . . .
The legislative department is by far the
strongest, and is constantly inclined to en-
croach upon the weaker branches of government and upon individual rights. . . . I
object to the Council of Revision as being
composed of the judiciary, who are not directly responsible to the people; I object to
it because it inevitably connects the judiciary with the intrigues and collisions of party
strife; because it tends to make our judges
politicians. . . . The community expect an
alteration of the legislative check, but not
an abandonment of the principle."

The veto power, thus supported, was

adopted by an immense majority. Upon this increase of the power of the Executive, Van Buren immediately demanded an increase of his responsibility to the people. "We have given him," said he, "the exclusive vote. As we increase the power of the Governor, we should also increase his responsibility. We should bring him more frequently before the people. In the exercise of the veto, which will only take place on important occasions, he will be supported, if he shall have acted manifestly for the public good. As we have vastly increased the power of the Executive, I concur in the desire to abridge his term. But how abridge it? We wish the people to have an opportunity of testing their governor's conduct, not by the feelings of temporary excitement, but by that sober second thought which is never wrong." And against triennial and annual elections he argued successfully for the term of two years.

The old Council of Revision, composed of the Supreme Judges and the Chancellor, had negatived the first bill for this convention; four or five men could ill resist the people, and the convention was resolved upon removing them from office. The generous nature of Van Buren was satisfied with taking from the judges the veto on legislative power. He pleaded against ejecting them from office. He pleaded that there existed no public reasons for the measure.

"Why, then, are we to adopt it? Certainly not from personal feelings. If personal feelings could or ought to influence us against the individual who would probably be most affected by the adoption of this amendment" (the reference was to William W. Van Ness), "I, above all others, should be excused for indulging them. Through my whole life I have been assailed from that quarter with hostility—political, professional, and personal; hostility which has been the most keen, active, and unyielding. But, sir, am I to avail myself of my situation as a representative of the people, sent here to make a constitution for them and their posterity, to indulge my individual resentments in the prostration of my private and political adversary? I trust it is unnecessary for me to say that I should forever despise myself if I could be capable of such conduct."

This freedom from passion won a temporary triumph over the opinion of the Assembly; on that day the opinion of Van Buren was sustained by a large majority; nor were the judges displaced till the entire reorganization of the system.

Another important subject on which the convention was called to act was the Council of Appointment. By the old system, the Assembly elected from the Senate a council of appointment; in the hands of this council and the Governor all the appointing power was centralized. Against this mighty engine of party centralization Van Buren brought in a report, opposing its renewal and every substitute for it. He desired to transfer the appointing power, in a great part, directly to the people, and to leave the nomination of justices of the peace to officers in the respective counties. On the inquiry whether sheriffs and justices of the peace might be directly elected by the people, Van Buren doubted.

"We do not deny," said he, "the competency of the people to make a proper choice. This argument has been unfairly and untruly stated. Those who oppose the election of justices, do not do so because they have any distrust of the people; but the officer elected would of necessity be acquainted with all who opposed and all who supported him. This would more or less bias his mind in favor of those to whom he owed his election; and even if it did not, it would excite jealousy and suspicion of unfairness prejudicial to the public peace."

The views of Van Buren were, for the most part, adopted; the convention provided for the election of sheriffs by the people ; but the appointment of justices of the peace was lodged for a time with the supervisors and county courts. A later amendment secured to the people of the several towns the immediate election of their own magistrates.

On political influence to be derived from the appointing power itself, few public men have relied so little as Van Buren. During the period when one of his warmest friends held the office of governor for more terms than one, I have the authority of that friend for saying that he never once made an application to him on the subject of appointments. His opinion was ever that patronage should as little as possible be concentrated at the seat of government, whether in the State or Nation; and referring to his conduct in the New York Convention, he, at a later day, in a letter to a convention in

Indiana, renewed the expression of his opinion. "When we cannot dispense with the offices,' he writes, "we must distribute as widely as possible the power of appointing to them. It is wise to reserve the selection of public officers, as far as is practicable and convenient, to the people themselves."

On the nineteenth day of September the convention entered upon the reform of the elective franchise. For this end the Republican party of New York had desired the call of the convention; for this end the Democratic farmers of Otsego had adopted Van Buren as their representative in that body; for this end Van Buren, at Albany, on the 4th of July, had sounded the keynote for those who demanded a government of all by all.

At that time more than one-half of the inhabitants of New York were excluded from full suffrage, and the popular mind demanded its extension; yet in electing the members of the convention, no one district demanded from its candidate a pledge to support the introduction of absolute universal suffrage. That subject was further embarrassed by the fact that slavery had not as yet wholly disappeared from the State of New York; that the process of emancipation was going forward under a general law; and that of colored people in the State there were about fifty thousand, of whom many were but just emerging from slavery.

The report from the Committee on Suffrage, as modified by the first vote of the convention, proposed to abolish the property qualification, and, after six months' residence, to confer the right of voting on every man who paid a tax, or served in the militia, or worked on the highway. "The scheme," said Sanford, "will embrace almost the whole male population of the State." None knew better than Van Buren how much opposition this radical measure would meet, alike within the convention and with-

out it; and he watched the issue with apprehension.

Stephen Van Rensselaer, one of the committee on the elective franchise, a moderate
Federalist and most estimable man, dissented from the report, desiring to confine the
suffrage to tax-payers who had been longer
resident in the State.

James Fairlie, another of the committee,
though a Republican, likewise dissented,
and was unwilling to extend the right of
suffrage to service in the militia and work
on the roads.

Ambrose Spencer spoke vehemently in
opposition to the report; he would not extend the franchise to "those who work in
factories, and are employed by wealthy individuals in the capacity of laborers. Under the notion that there is a call for extending the right of suffrage, this report
goes to the most extravagant length."

Erastus Root objected to the report:
" There is danger of extending the right of

suffrage too far;" and moved the restriction which, on a subsequent day, he defended. "I do not desire," said he, "any strolling voters nor any broomstick voters. I only want those who may contribute to the defence of the country. They should be armed and equipped according to law, before they should be privileged to vote. . . . Those excluded will be a very small proportion, and not of the description of people who are of any value."

The opponents of abolishing freehold restrictions took encouragement; and on the 22d of September, Ambrose Spencer, in direct antagonism to Van Buren, proposed by an amendment to retain, in the election of the Senate, the old property distinction. "The sober sense of the community," he insisted, had not demanded "deep and dangerous innovation." "Are we jealous," continued he, "of property, that we should leave it unprotected? To the beneficence and liberality of those who have property we

owe all the embellishments and the comforts and blessings of life. Who build our
churches? Who erect our hospitals? Who
raise our school-houses? Those who have
property. And are they not entitled to the
regard and fostering protection of our laws
and Constitution? ... Let us take care,
whilst we nominally give the right of voting
to a particular description of our citizens,
that we do not in reality give it to their employers. The man who feeds, clothes, and
lodges another has a real and absolute control over his will. Say what we may, the
man who is dependent upon another for his
subsistence is not an independent man, and
he will vote in subservience to his dictation."

The debate continued through several
days.

James Kent, the venerable chancellor,
lent the influence of his endowments, his
weight of character, and the personal qualities which made him the delight of private
life, to the side of restriction. " The Sen-

ate," said he, "should continue, as hereto-
fore, the representative of the landed interest, and exempted from the control of universal suffrage. . . . By the report before us,
we propose to annihilate at one stroke all
those property distinctions, and to bow before the idol of universal suffrage. That
extreme democratic principle, when applied
to the legislative and executive departments
of government, has been regarded with ter-
ror by the wise men of every age. . . . If we
are like other races of men, with similar
follies and vices, then I greatly fear that our
posterity will have reason to deplore in
sackcloth and ashes the delusion of the
day. . . . I wish to preserve our Senate as
the representative of the landed interest. . . .
I wish them to be always enabled to say that
their freeholders cannot be taxed without
their consent. . . . The apprehended danger
from the experiment of universal suffrage,
applied to the whole legislative department,
is no dream of the imagination; it is too

6

mighty an excitement for the moral constitution of men to endure.   The tendency of
universal suffrage is to jeopard the rights of
property and the principles of liberty. . . .
The growth of the city of New York is
enough to startle and awaken those who are
pursuing the ignis fatuus of universal suffrage. . . . We are destined to become a
great manufacturing as well as commercial
State.   We have already numerous and
prosperous factories of one kind or another; and one master-capitalist, with his one
hundred apprentices and journeymen and
agents and dependants, will bear down at
the polls an equal number of farmers of
small estates in his vicinity, who cannot
safely unite for their common defence.
Large manufacturing and mechanical estab-
lishments can act in an instant, with the
unity and efficacy of disciplined troops.   It
is against such combinations, among others,
that I think we ought to give to the freeholders, or those who have interest in land,

one branch of the Legislature for their asylum and their comfort. Universal suffrage, once granted, can never be recalled. There is no retrograde step in the rear of democracy. However mischievous the precedent may be in its consequences, or however fatal in its effects, universal suffrage never can be recalled or checked but by the strength of the bayonet. We stand, therefore, at this moment on the brink of fate, on the very edge of the precipice. If we let go our present hold on the Senate, we commit our proudest hopes and our most precious interests to the waves."

Van Vechten argued that property must be privileged, or it never would be secure.

Tompkins, the Democratic president of the convention, replied: " Property, when compared with our other essential rights, is insignificant and trifling. Life, liberty, and the pursuit of happiness, not of property, are set forth in the Declaration of Independence as cardinal objects. . . . How was

the late war sustained? Who filled the
ranks of your armies? Not the priesthood,
not the men of wealth, not the speculators.
The former were preaching sedition, and
the latter decrying the credit of the Government to fatten on its spoil. And yet the
very men who were led on to battle had no
vote to give for their commander-in-chief. . . .
We give to property too much influence. It
is not that which mostly gives independence.
Independence consists more in the structure
of the mind and in the qualities of the heart.
We should look to the protection of him
who has personal security and personal liberty at stake."

Elisha Williams, in a long speech, advocated the property qualification. "And
who are these people," he demanded, "who
are to aid the freeholders in electing their
Senate? . . . Sir, they are the ring-streaked
and speckled population of our large towns
and cities, comprising people of every kin-
dred and tongue. They bring with them

the habits, vices, political creeds, and nation-
alities of every section of the globe; they
have fled from oppression, if you please, and
have habitually regarded sovereignty and
tyranny as identified; they are men whose
wants, if not whose vices, have sent them
from other States and countries, to seek
bread by service, if not by plunder; whose
means and habits, whose best kind of ambition, and only sort of industry, all forbid
their purchasing in the country and tilling
the soil."

The 25th of September was the memorable day on which the essential question of
free suffrage was to be decided. On that
morning Van Buren rose to speak for the
government of all by all. The whole assembly listened intently, and the gravity of
a subject which affected the rights of more
than half the men of New York gave so-
lemnity to the scene.

His first words were employed to allay
the panic which it had been attempted to

raise.   He paid a just tribute "to the known
candor and purity of character" of Chancellor Kent, but calmly put aside his unfounded fears and apprehensions. "If a stranger,"
said Van Buren, "had heard the discussions
on this subject, and had been unacquainted
with the character of our people, and the
character and standing of those who find it
their duty to oppose this measure, he might
well have supposed that we were on the
point of prostrating with lawless violence
one of the fairest and firmest pillars of the
Government."

Appealing to the institutions of other
States, especially of New England and Ohio,
he proved the security of industry and property, of civil and of religious liberty, without
freehold representation.

He next treated the question as it affected property and as it affected freedom. The
personal property in the State which was
the subject of taxation was about one hundred and fifty millions of dollars; the real

estate was valued at two hundred and fifty-six millions. Would the advocates for a representation of property exclude their personal property from representation in the Senate?

"By the census of 1814," he continued, "it appeared that of one hundred and sixty-three thousand electors, seventy-five thousand are freeholders under two hundred and fifty dollars, and all of them householders. . . . Shall this class of men, composed of mechanics, professional men, and small land-holders, be excluded entirely from all representation in that branch of the Legislature which has equal power to originate all bills, a negative on all laws, and, as a court of last resort, is intrusted with the life, liberty, and property of every one of our citizens? This is the grievance under which so great a portion of the people of this State have hitherto labored. It is to relieve them from this injustice and this oppression that the convention has been called.

"There are two words which came into common use with our Revolutionary struggle; words which contain an abridgment of our political rights; words which, at the day, had a talismanic effect; which led our fathers from the bosom of their families to the tented field; which, for seven long years of toil and suffering, kept them to their arms, and finally conducted them to a glorious triumph. They are, taxation and representation. Nor did they lose their influence with the close of that struggle. They are never heard in our halls of legislation without bringing to our recollections the consecrated feelings of those who won our liberties.

"Apply for a moment the principles they inculcate to the question under consideration. Are those of your citizens represented whose voices are never heard in your Senate? Are those citizens in any degree represented or heard in the formation of your courts of justice, from the highest to the lowest? Is, then, representation in one branch of the Legislature, which by itself can do nothing, anything more than a shadow? Is it not emphatically keeping the word of promise to the ear and breaking it to the hope? Is it not even less than the virtual representation with which our fathers were attempted to be appeased by their oppressors? It is even so; and if so, can we, as long as this distinction is retained, hold up our heads, and, without blushing, pretend to be the advocates for that special canon of political rights, that taxation and representation are, and ever should be, indissoluble? I think not.

"In whose name and for whose benefit are we called upon to disappoint the just expectations of our constituents, and to persevere in what I cannot but regard as a violation of principle? In the name and for the security of farmers! This is, indeed, acting in an imposing name, and they who use it know full well that it is so! It is

the boast, the pride, and the security of this
nation that she has in her bosom a body
of men who, for sobriety, integrity, industry, and patriotism, are unequalled by the
cultivators of the earth in any other part
of the known world. Nay, more : to com-
pare them with men of similar pursuits in
other countries is to degrade them. And
woful must be our degeneracy before anything which may be supposed to affect the
interests of the farmers of this country can
be listened to with indifference by those
who govern us.

" I yield to no man in respect for this
invaluable class of our citizens, or in zeal
for their support; but is the allegation that
we are violating the wishes and tampering
with the security of the farmers founded in
fact ? Who have hitherto constituted the
majority of the voters of the State ? The
farmers. Who called for and insisted upon
the convention ? Farmers and freeholders.
Who passed the law admitting those who

were not electors to a free participation in
the decision of the question of convention
or no convention? and also in the choice
of delegates to this body? A Legislature
a majority of whom were farmers, and probably every one of them freeholders of the
value of two hundred and fifty dollars and
upwards! The farmers of this State have, by
an overwhelming majority, admitted those
who were not freeholders to a full participation with themselves in every stage of
this great effort to amend our Constitution
and to ameliorate the condition of the people. Ought I, then, to be told that they
will be disappointed in their expectations
when they find that, by the provisions of
the Constitution, as amended, a great proportion of their fellow-citizens are enfranchised and released from fetters which they
themselves had done all in their power to
loosen? I do not believe it.

"The farmers look for such an event.
They earnestly desire it. Whatever rav-

ages the possession of power may have
made in the breasts of others, the farmers,
at least, have shown that they can feel
power without forgetting right. If anything
can render this invaluable class of men
dearer and more estimable than they were,
it is this magnanimous sacrifice which they
make on the altar of principle, by consent-
ing to admit their fellow-citizens, not so
highly favored as themselves by fortune, to
an equal participation in the blessings of a
free government."

Turning from freeholders, he next addressed himself to "the men of property,"
and, expressing his determination neither
to hamper the rich nor tread upon the
poor, he dropped the distinction made between real and personal estate, and pro-
ceeded to demonstrate that the proposed
restriction on suffrage offered no new security to property; that the principles of
order and good government in the people,
and the sense in legislators of their imme-

diate responsibility to the people, are the securities against agrarian laws, extravagance, and unequal taxation ; that every effort at procuring a representation of individual property, or of the property of sections of the State, has been, and from the nature of the case ever will be, delusive.

To the argument derived from precedent and the theoretic opinion of the men of the Revolution, he replied that Constitutions develop themselves with the growing opinion of a nation, as a tree shapes itself from its inherent life. " A full and perfect experience has proved the fallacy of the fearful forebodings of the patriots who made our Constitution ; and we are now called upon to adopt the exploded notion, and on that ground to disfranchise nearly a moiety, if not a majority, of our citizens." In the spirit of hope he alluded to the fears which hung round the venerable Franklin, the lamented Hamilton, and even Madison —fears of which experience has proved the

fallacy. " Having the records of experience before me," he continued, " I will be
governed by them."

After demonstrating that the attempted
representation of property in the Senate
would be delusive, he proved that "sound
policy dictated the abandonment of it by
the possessors of property themselves."

Williams, of Columbia, who had insulted
the name of Jefferson, he rebuked for re-
taining prejudices that seemed immortal,
against "the man who had done his country the greatest service, and who at that
moment occupied more space in the public
mind than any other private citizen in the
world."

Chief-justice Spencer, who pleaded for
disfranchising persons employed in manu-
factories, because they would be influenced
by their employers, he caught on the horns
of this dilemma: "If they are so influenced,
they will be enlisted on the side of property which you propose to promote; if they

are independent of their employers, they will be safe depositaries of the right."

And as the same speaker had foreboded, from an extended suffrage, the introduction into America of the corruption of rotten boroughs, Van Buren answered, " The cause of those corruptions is this: the representation of Great Britain is a representation of territory, and not of men."

To Chancellor Kent his words were: " If I could possibly believe that from an extended suffrage there could result any portion of the calamitous consequences which have been so feelingly portrayed, I would be the last man in society to vote for it. But believing, as I conscientiously do, that those fears are altogether unfounded, hoping and expecting the happiest results from the abolition of the freehold qualification, and hoping, too, that caution and circumspection will preside over the settlement of the general right of suffrage which is hereafter to be made, and knowing, besides, that this State, in abolishing the freehold qualifications, will be but uniting herself in the march of principle which has already prevailed in every State of the Union, except two or three, including the royal charter of Rhode Island, I shall cheerfully record my vote against the amendment."

It is related by Hammond, the historian of New York, that "the speech of Van Buren was greatly superior to any other which was made on that vitally important question; it was a dignified, philosophical, statesmanlike view of the subject; logical and eloquent." "Had this been the only public service of Van Buren," adds the same historian, "this single argument would have entitled him to take rank among the most shining orators and able statesmen of the age." I have been assured by those who well recollect the circumstances, that the effect of this powerful and well-reasoned speech upon the convention was conceived to be decisive of the question; yet Van

Ness rose, and in the course of his remarks spoke as follows: " What is the character of the poor ? Generally speaking, vice and poverty go hand in hand. By an irresisti- ble decree of Providence, it is pronounced, ' The poor ye have always with you'; peo- ple who have no interest in your institu- tions, no fixedness of habitation, no proper- ty to defend;" and he insisted on limiting the franchise to freeholders.

" The poor!" retorted Samuel Young; " I say, and that, too, with emphasis, that they ought not to be excluded. They are the soundest, the most honest, and most incor- ruptible part of your population."

The vote was taken. Van Buren found himself, on that happy day, one of a hun- dred, while his adversaries counted but nineteen. Well has it been said, Peace has its victories. The progress of civilization is fast diminishing the frequency of wars; the harvest of glory is now to be gathered on the battle-field of thought; and when,

7

within the great central State, has a might-
ier battle been fought or a more momentous victory won, than on the day which
saw the freeholders of the State of New
York abdicate their privilege with hearty
good-will, and the full, undivided sovereignty was transferred from the territory of
New York to its men?

The consequences of this example are
not yet fully developed. New York City
has risen to be one of the three most opulent and populous cities on the globe; and
the interior of the State has developed such
greatness that few of the States in the
cultivated world surpass her in resources.
Her population increases; schools and col-
leges are fostered; highways, railroads, and
canals intersect the country; public credit
is sacredly maintained; a river turned from
its source assists to supply her chief city
with water; a humane system of prison dis-
cipline has made her the teacher of kings
and nations; the spirit of philanthropy soft-

ens the old penal code. Her ships go round the world; and wherever they go they carry evidence of the safety of property, the increase of wealth, the security of rights, the multiplication of comforts, the diffusion of happiness, the progress of letters. And when the nations gaze with astonishment, and ask under what institution men have been quickened to achieve these results, New York answers with a voice that every year is more and more listened to through the world, that they are due to the all-pervading genius of universal suffrage.

Immediately after the decision of the convention against a property qualification for the exercise of the suffrage, a seemingly strange result followed. No mode of defeating free suffrage remained, except by giving to the amendments a character which should offend the people. Columbia County had sent to the convention William W. Van Ness and Elisha Williams, the former

then a judge of the Supreme Court, and the
other an eminent lawyer—two of the ablest
men of the State. They represented Van
Buren's native county in that body, and had
been from his youth his competitors and
rivals in every form. No two members of
the convention were more bitterly hostile
to every extension of the suffrage. But of
a sudden they and others, who, with them,
had vehemently sustained the freehold qualification of the voter, urged the convention
in debate, though not by their votes, to go
to the extreme on the other side; and when
New York was just abolishing slavery, Judge
Van Ness favored a motion that would give
the right of voting to all residents of three
years, without distinction of color, even to
the slave on the moment of his emancipation. The number of negro votes that would
have thus been created was computed at
many thousands. Van Buren, who knew
most thoroughly the character and opinions
of his antagonists, grew more cautious than

ever. " He believed," writes Hammond,
"that Mr. Williams and the gentleman with
whom Mr. Williams acted were desirous of
defeating all alterations in the Constitution,
and he suspected that their object was to
encourage General Root and his friends to
push their notions of enlarging the right of
suffrage to such an extent as would induce
the people to condemn the whole of the proceedings of the convention. Was there not
danger," adds the same disinterested wit-
ness, " that by a union of action of the ul-
tras of both parties, a result might be produced of which the people at that time
would not approve?" Van Buren put the
convention on their guard against such " a
course of action." " The gentleman from
Columbia," said he, referring to Elisha Williams, and giving warning to the convention,
" is not perhaps so much interested in the
amendment as myself, since that gentleman
expressed a belief, a few days ago, that we
have already made the Constitution worse ;

and he probably would not regret to see us go so far as to have all the amendments rejected by the people." And while he advocated an easy and simple method by which future amendments could be made, he avowed himself satisfied with what was certainly gained, and was willing, for the time, if by such forbearance he could conciliate unanimity, to extend the franchise no further than to all who paid any tax, however small, or performed military service, or, being householders, had worked on the highway. He would not consent to bestow suffrage "on every one, black or white"; and in the debate on the amendment which gave the right of voting to all residents, including the numérous negro population, Van Buren spoke against such extension. "We are hazarding everything," were his words, "by going to such lengths in the amendments. The people will never sanction them."

The convention, finding itself embarrassed in its opinions, referred the whole subject to a select committee of thirteen, and Samuel Young, as its chairman, soon made a report.

To the black man the committee extended the suffrage if he possessed a freehold of the clear value of two hundred and fifty dollars; otherwise he was exempted from taxation and had no vote. Kent was unwilling to see the blacks disfranchised, and the door eternally barred against them. " The proviso," said he, though for another cause he voted against it, " will not cut them off from all hope. . . . The prospect of participating in the right of suffrage will have a tendency to make them industrious and frugal." Van Buren gave his support to the restriction on negro suffrage. " I voted," said he, " against a tõtal and unqualified exclusion; for I would not draw a revenue from them, and yet deny to them the right of suffrage. But this proviso meets my approbation. It exempts them from taxation until they have qualified themselves to vote, and holds out inducements to industry.". " The proviso," said Young, " is the result of compromise. . . . If it is rejected, I shall move to exclude the blacks altogether." The proviso was sustained by a great majority within the convention, and quieted agitation throughout the State.

Little difficulty remained in establishing the right of suffrage for the whites. The qualification of military service, omitted by the committee, was supported by Van Buren, and prevailed. An effort was made by Jacob R. Van Rensselaer, of Columbia County, to require from a voter the possession of property, real and personal, to the amount of fifty dollars. He wished " to exclude those who may feel, perhaps, too strong a desire to violate private rights for the justification of their cupidity."

Up rose Olney Briggs, a plain and upright patriot from Schoharie. "We have come," said he, "to universal suffrage, sir, and I want we should fix it in the face of the instrument, sir. Gentlemen wish to get away from it; they endeavor to evade it, sir. This distinction will help to weaken the breach. When we get to such a population as the gentlemen have described, our Constitution will be good for nothing, sir. We must carry the strong arm of the law to the cradle, sir, and let the rising generation know that we have established the principle of universal suffrage, sir, that they may prepare themselves accordingly, and qualify themselves to live under it, sir."

Van Buren, Fairlie, and others, spoke on the same side, but not at length; they said that "the question had been fully settled several days ago," and Van Rensselaer's motion was promptly voted down.

Ezekiel Bacon, of Oneida, who was a friend to freehold qualification, and had yet afterwards voted to bestow the franchise on all residents, except actual paupers, whether white or black, if twenty-one years of age, now opposed the highway qualification. Van Buren, who, for conciliation, had at first been willing to limit that qualification to householders and had carried the convention with him for that limitation, once more exposed the former conduct of Bacon and Van Ness, in vibrating from one extreme to the other, and would now listen to no compromise whatever. " Under all circumstances," said he, " I shall be well satisfied with the right of suffrage as it will now be established, and will give it my zealous support, as well in my capacity of delegate as in that of citizen." And the Republican party, with great unanimity, joined in extending the suffrage to every male citizen of twenty-one years who had resided within the State for one year, within the county six months, and had paid a tax or done military duty, or performed labor on the highways. Four or five years afterwards, with Van Buren's approbation, his political friends, being a majority of the people, made the vote still more simple, requiring only residence. The amendments proposed by the convention were adopted by the people at the polls almost by acclamation. In one short year this momentous revolution was conceived and consummated, so warily as not to excite astonishment or alarm, so thoroughly as to stand forth an example to the human race. So frequently are great things done in America for freedom, that we almost cease to applaud, even where the highest benefits are conferred, under the blessed influences of tranquillity and law.

The enemies of all extension of suffrage, nourishing their spleen by insulated words taken down by a reporter who declared Van Buren's utterance so rapid that it was impossible to do him justice, have had the nicest feelings of most sensitive regrets for his good name as a Republican, because he did not hazard everything by language which might have generated alarm and helped them in their attempt to defeat all amendments. Nothing in his public career so much endeared Van Buren to his party in New York as his conduct in this convention. Eighteen years afterwards he made a journey through the State, and William L. Marcy, then its governor, recounted it publicly among the causes " of the kind reception which everywhere awaited him." At Batavia he was greeted with heartiest hospitality for the various measures which he had proposed and supported; above all, for the measures which enfranchised " the great mass of inhabitants of those western counties."

In Otsego, the county of his constituents, thousands gathered around him to greet his presence. " Of the most consequential acts of your public life," said their appointed speaker, " one is too important to be omitted. I refer to your support and advocacy of the principle of universal suffrage in the convention which formed our present Constitution." And amid cheers of approbation from the assembled multitude, in the name of the " rich, as well as of the thousands of enfranchised poor," he tendered the thanks of all classes to their former representative for his services in doing away with " exclusive rights" and " abolishing a distinction opposed to liberal principles."

CHAPTER IV.

EIGHT YEARS IN THE SENATE OF THE UNITED STATES: 1821–1829.

ON the sixth day of February, 1821, the Democratic Legislature which initiated constitutional reform in the State of New York elected Van Buren to the Senate of the United States. He took his seat in that body, sustained by the confiding attachment of his constituents.

The Government, under the apparent extinction of party spirit, had been verging from the simplicity of republican policy. The next eight years ripened the public opinion which afterwards guided the administration of the country. In free governments the enlightened conviction of the people is the source, the condition, and the guarantee of permanency to just legislation, and he that assists in forming a right national opinion renders his country the truest service.

On entering the Senate, Van Buren was made a member of the Finance Committee, as well as of the Committee on the Judiciary. Of the latter he was soon elected chairman. He retained that post during his service in Congress, and took a leading part in all questions which involved the interpretation of the Constitution.

At that time the strict construction of the Constitution was giving way to arbitrary interpretation; the subject of internal improvements was the constant theme of political discussion, and upon that question hinged the politics of the country. The opinion was openly and formally avowed, that "it is unwise and impolitic for the Government to hasten the payment of the public debt"; that "any surplus in the Treasury would be more usefully employed in the internal improvement of the country."

To this impulse Monroe began to yield, and a thinly settled Western territory looked to the General Government for means of communication with their old homes. Friends of the Union favored grants to promote domestic intercourse. The most discreet of our retired statesmen watched with lively interest the progress of national roads and canals, and Madison, beholding in them bonds of union, was fond of remarking that they "dovetailed the States." The manufacturers and merchants required lines of communication between the two great oceans; the farmers needed better avenues to the great markets of the world; public opinion became impatient of constitutional scruples and clamored for action.

The opportunity of winning the favor of States tempted ambition, and schemes were rapidly formed to thread the mountain passes, to form lines of connection and internal navigation from the ports on the Atlantic coast. Nor were projects of grandeur and truly national importance alone brought forward. Whenever a canal was planned the aid of the General Government was invoked; and even turnpikes beginning and ending within a State, under the notion that they might be travelled upon by men passing through one State to another, were claimed to have a national character, and a right to solicit the General Government to become a share-holder in the risks and profits of their construction. Every grant was sure to generate a brood of new demands; and members of Congress favored projects which, from their number and extent, would have required an outlay of hundreds of millions of dollars.

The vast expenditure in which this system would have involved the nation was the least objection to it. "If the national Government should construct the roads and canals throughout the Union, an excess of centralized power would ensue; the freedom of our States, which is the happiest achieve-

8

ment of modern civilization in the method
of government, would be crushed in central
confusion. But centralization is akin to
despotism. Within the State it is the freedom of the individual that makes possible
the government of all by all; within the
federal system the individuality and freedom of each State can alone restrain the
General Government from the assumption
of arbitrary power. To confine the system
of internal improvements by the General
Government within the bounds of the Constitution was therefore demanded of those
who desired and labored to insure the success of the American experiment.

The assumption by the General Government of a universal scheme of internal improvements would have corrupted our Constitution in the very sources of its life. It
would have fastened upon us that brand of
monopoly, the restrictive system, and delayed infinitely the approximation to the
liberal commercial policy which springs nat-

urally out of republican institutions, and which America, from regard to itself, independent of all external influences, should desire to establish.

It would have involved the country in new debts, and so have entailed on it the financial policy that belongs to public indebtment.

It would have opened opportunities for lavish expenditures, corruption, and favoritism, and have increased public patronage to an unbounded extent.

It would have diminished the power of the people; for the nearer a subject is kept to the people, the more easily can it be controlled; but when the turnpike before the farmer's door depends on Congress or the Cabinet at Washington, the opportunity of local supervision is lost.

The progress of this dangerous policy was already exciting alarm, and even Jefferson suffered his serene mind, though but for a moment, to be clouded with gloomy forebodings.

Against this system Van Buren assisted to form public opinion at the North. In the Legislature of New York he had won for himself honor as the advocate of internal improvements within his native State by its own authority and resources. His devotion to the cause of internal improvements under their proper auspices singled him out to lead debate, and to guide opinion in favor of a strict construction of the Constitution.

In January, 1824, Van Buren invoked the attention of the Senate to the tendency of the National Legislature, by its own construction, to enlarge its powers over this subject; he reviewed the conflict of opinion between the executive and legislative departments, and proposed amendments to the Constitution, for the purpose of defining powers and setting an impassable barrier to encroachments.

In December, 1825, he renewed the discussion, and proposed the resolution, " that

Congress does not possess the power to make roads and canals within the respective States;" nor would he assent to the exercise of any such power till it should be defined by an amendment of the Constitution. His movement on this subject called forth the applause of the venerable Macon, the Senator from North Carolina, whose eyes would fill with tears when he viewed the rapid change which the character of the Government had undergone in the interval between his entrance on public life and his old age. It was a new era. The State that had been the home of Alexander Hamilton and Gouverneur Morris, presented itself on the floor of the Senate as the advocate of the restraining principles of the Constitution.

In April, 1826, on a question of an appropriation for a canal, Van Buren said: "The aid of this Government can only be afforded to these objects of improvement in three ways: by making a road or canal

and assuming jurisdiction; by leaving jurisdiction to the respective States; or by making an appropriation without doing either.
In my opinion, the General Government
have no right to do either."

Congress was urged to subscribe to the
Dismal Swamp Canal.

"I will not vote for the bill," said Van
Buren, in May, 1826, "for I do not believe
that this Government possesses the constitutional power to make these canals, or to
grant money to make them." And then,
branching off into the general question of
subscription on the part of Government to
canals, he uttered a warning, not then listened to, saying: "Even where the power
exists, the mode of aiding by a Government
subscription for stock is the last one to be
adopted; abuses would creep in, and, in
nine cases out of ten, deception be practised." "In the State of New York," he in-
cidentally added, "we have had full experience of this in the application for charters

for banks. Plausible pretences were set up that the State would thereby be benefited; but, in the end, public opinion is decidedly against these practices, and the last Legislature, to their honor, has refused all applications of this description."

When it was urged against him that the repeated action of Congress had settled the constitutionality of the practice, he entered his protest against the admission of the doctrine, insisting that repeated action can never sanctify a wrong interpretation of an instrument of which Congress has no power to change even a word.

And when an accidental majority proposed to commit the country irrevocably, by making the United States a joint-stock partner in canals, with permanent liabilities, he, in May, 1826, made the general declaration of his own creed, which was the true creed of republicanism.

" I shall resist to all intents and purposes the idea that the acts of this Congress are to bind me and my constituents forever hereafter. The power of repeal cannot be wrested by one Congress from all its successors."

The majority in the Senate was against him; but Van Buren persevered. His effort was not followed by immediate action; but it assisted in the formation of public opinion. In a few short years he had the satisfaction, being in the Cabinet, to find the opinions he had maintained in the Senate adopted by Andrew Jackson, and unfolded, and enforced, and carried through the country to the convictions of the people by the Maysville veto.

The same hostility to centralization had uniformly dictated Van Buren's opinions on the subject of the disposition of the national domain. To facilitate actual settlement and to withdraw the land-offices were always his leading objects. " The subject of the public lands," said he, in May, 1826, " is becoming daily more and more interesting;

it extends the patronage of the Government over the States in which they are situated to a great extent; it subjects them to an unwise and unprofitable dependence on the Federal Government.... No man can render the country a greater service than he who should devise some plan by which the United States may be relieved from the ownership of this property by some equitable mode. I will vote for a proposition to vest the lands in the States in which they stand, on some just and equitable terms as relate to the other States in the confederacy. I hope that, after having full information on the subject, we shall be able to effect that great object. I believe that if those lands were disposed of at once to the several States it would be satisfactory to all."

Van Buren struggled to secure to the people alone the election of their chief magistrate. He desired to take from Congress, and preserve inviolably and exclu-

sively to the people themselves, the right
of electing their President and Vice-president.   To this end he proposed an amendment of the Constitution, by which the election should never come to the House of
Representatives, but, in case of division on
the first ballot, be referred again to the in-
corruptible millions.

The proposed method is eminently democratic.   Cabals and factions may hereafter
succeed in bringing before the people many
names, and often, on the first ballot, there
may be a division of votes.   Factions are
composed of men drawn together by interests, and their interests may be several, and
may in a degree be antagonistic.   But the
government of all by all, resting on princi-
ciple and truth, is adverse to division, because truth is the same always and everywhere.   The government of all by all, therefore, desires always the opportunity for
popular union.   Again, it is the nature of
the party of the few to wish to contract as

much as possible the numbers of those on whose counsel it depends; the government of all by all, on the contrary, desires to gather its decision from the largest and most comprehensive expression of the popular intelligence. As the friend to popular power, and as the friend to union, Van Buren was desirous, in case of a failure of an attempt at an election of President, to refer the subject again to the people, and to keep the decision within their will.

Equally friendly to the government of all by all was the mode by which this was to be accomplished. " I have," said he, "prepared a resolution which requires the contemplated division of the States into districts, to be coextensive with the number of electors." And on the eighth day of May, 1826, pledging himself to persistency in urging the proposed reform, he added: "There is no one point on which the people of the United States are more perfectly united than upon the propriety, not to say

indispensable necessity, of taking the election of President from the House of Representatives. The experience under the Constitution as it stands, as well formerly as
recently, has produced that impression, and
I consider the vote of the House of Representatives as the strongest manifestation
of its existence. In that respect it will be
of value, but beyond that it can produce no
results. Although it can, I think, be satis-
factorily shown that the small States would,
if nothing more was done, be better off than
they are under the Constitution as it stands,
still all experience has shown that they do
not think so. There is no reason to believe
that they will ever consent to give up the
power they now have without an equivalent;
without a resort to the principle upon which
the Constitution was founded—that of compromise. The equivalent with which they
would be satisfied, with which they ought
to be satisfied, is the breaking up of the
consolidated strength of the large States

by the establishment of the district system."

Thus did Van Buren, the representative
of the largest and most commercial State
in the Union, raise his voice in favor of
electing the President by the district system. In case of no election on the first
ballot, his plan proposed that the people
themselves, in the districts, should on a second trial make an election between the two
highest candidates.

The amendment cuts up by the roots all
combinations between the great States ; it
divides the whole Union into single electoral districts, thus giving to the minorities
in the several States the greatest possible
chance of being represented.

In the course of the discussion of this
subject Van Buren gave strong utterance
to his abhorrence of every tendency in our
government to centralization, raising his
voice against " a completely consolidated
government," which the fathers of the coun-

try had so much dreaded, and which, if effected, coming generations would so much
deplore. " However ardent," he added, " my
attachment to the Federal Government, and
however anxious I may be to sustain it in
the exercise of the powers given to it by
the Constitution—and in that respect I will
go as far as any man ought to go—I am
unwilling to destroy, or even to release, its
dependence on the State governments. . . .
That qualified dependence of the Federal
Government is their strong arm of defence
to protect them against future abuses."

Thus did Van Buren vindicate the principle of the union of Free States, giving
in his adhesion to the federative principle
which, like that of democratic power, is, let
us hope, destined to make the .tour of the
globe. Federative States, federative government; the nation to be formed by the
free union of separate integral parts that
in their union preserve individuality and
local sovereignty—this is the rule of mod-

ern civilization which the cultivated nations of the world are slowly learning, but which, as surely as the principles of inductive reason shall be applied universally to public affairs, will make a conquest of nations, and carry to the Old World, as well as diffuse throughout the New, the well-ordered system of federal republics—of people individually free, having life and organization in all their parts, and combining separate living States in the higher life of a confederated people.

The same care was present to Van Buren in arranging the changes to be adopted in the judiciary system in consequence of the very rapid increase of the country. The Constitution of the United States forbids each State to pass laws impairing the obligation of contracts. The object of this prohibition was a special one; a construction has been given to it which brings before the General Government questions relating to a free bridge and the monopoly of a ferry, to trust funds for local purposes, extending the jurisdiction of the national courts so far that, unless the tendency is arrested, the channel of justice with federal courts must become choked up by the multiplicity of business, and the designs of its creation be defeated. Good-sense, therefore, requires that the spirit of centralization should, above all places, not find its abode in the supreme judicial court; and the very nature of popular justice imperatively demands that every question should, as far as possible, be decided by the nearest tribunal—by juries and courts of the vicinage. The disinclination which democracy entertains of the too great extension of the powers of the Supreme' Court of the United States must, with the increase of our country, prevail even in the minds of those who will yield their desires for such extension with unmingled reluctance.

On this subject the views of Van Buren, as expressed in the Senate of the United

States in April, 1826, convey the judgment
and the apprehensions of his constituents.

"It has been justly observed elsewhere
that there exists not upon earth, and there
never did exist, a judicial tribunal clothed
with powers so various and so important as
the Supreme Court. . . .

"Not only are the acts of the National
Legislature subject to its review, but it
stands as the umpire between the conflicting powers of the General and State governments. That wide field of debatable
ground between those rival powers is
claimed to be subject to the exclusive and
absolute dominion of the Supreme Court.
The discharge of this solemn duty has not
been unfrequent, and certainly not unin-
teresting. In virtue of this power, we have
seen it holding for naught the statutes of
powerful States, which had received the
deliberate sanction not only of their Legislatures, but of their highest judicatories,
composed of men venerable in years, of un-

9

sullied purity and unrivalled talents—statutes on the faith of which immense estates
had been invested, and the inheritance of
the widow and the orphan was suspended.
You have seen such statutes abrogated by
the decision of this court, and those who
had confided in the wisdom and power of
the State authorities plunged in irreme-
diable ruin—decisions final in their effect,
and ruinous in their consequences. . . .

" By the Constitution of the United
States, the States are prohibited from passing 'any law impairing the obligation of
contracts.' This brief provision has given
the jurisdiction of the Supreme Court a
tremendous sweep. . . .

" I must not be understood as complain-
ing of the exercise of this jurisdiction by
the Supreme Court, or to pass upon the
correctness of their decisions. The authority has been given to them, and this is not
the place to question its exercise. But this
I will say, that if the question of conferring

it was now presented for the first time, I should unhesitatingly say that the people of the States might with safety be left to their own Legislatures and the protection of their own courts. . . .

" There are those—and they are neither small in number nor light in character— who think that the uniform tendency of the political decisions of the Supreme Court has been to strengthen the arm of the General Government and to weaken the States. . . .

" This has become a subject on which it is difficult to speak without unpleasantly encountering the strong opinions entertained on different sides of the question. On the one hand, expressions of distrust and dissatisfaction are heard, of a character so strongly marked as to defeat their object and recoil upon their authors ; on the other, a sentiment, I had almost said of idolatry for the Supreme Court, has grown up, which claims for its members an almost entire exemption from the fallibilities of our nature, and arraigns with unsparing bitterness the motives of all who have the temerity to look with inquisitive eyes into this consecrated sanctuary of the law. So powerful has this sentiment become, such strong hold has it taken upon the press of this country, that it requires not a little share of firmness in a public man, however imperious may be his duty, to express sentiments that conflict with it. It is, nevertheless, correct that in this, as in almost every other case, the truth is to be found in a just medium of the subject. But to the sentiment which claims for the judges so great a share of exemption from the feelings that govern the conduct of other men, and for the court the character of being the safest depository of political power, I do not subscribe. I have been brought up in an opposite faith, and all my experience has confirmed me in its correctness. In my legislation upon this subject I will act in conformity to those opinions. I believe the judges of the Supreme Court (great and good men as I cheerfully concede them to be) are subject to the same infirmities, influenced by the same passions, and operated upon by the same causes that good and great men are in other situations. I believe they have as much of the *esprit de corps* as other men; those who think otherwise form an erroneous estimate of human nature; and if they act upon that estimate will, soon or late, become sensible of their delusion. . . .

"With feelings for the General Government, as I humbly hope, purely catholic, I firmly believe, and my daily experience confirms that conviction, that much, very much of the present prosperity of the country and its institutions depends upon the successful action of the State governments, and that the preservation of their rightful powers is the *sine qua non* of our future welfare. I will not, therefore, give my assent to any measure which may still further disqualify the States to sustain themselves in those collisions of power which are unavoidable, and in which the situation of the parties is already so unequal. I believe a different disposition of the judges of the Supreme Court from that provided by this bill would have such effect, and I am, therefore, most decidedly opposed to it."

In like manner, Van Buren endeavored to confine the subject of prospective insolvent laws exclusively to the States.

Against imprisonment for debt, which he had brought the Senate of New York to condemn as a relic of a barbarous age and at war with all improvement, he had continued his warfare in the Senate of the United States, desiring to concentrate against the enormity the legislation and the opinion of the united country. In January, 1823, at a time when many regarded the dictates of humanity as the clamor of dishonesty for security, Van Buren, to remove all objections to the measure, offered various amendments to protect the creditor against the fraudulent concealment of property. Having guarded against reasonable objections, in March, 1825, he pleaded earnestly, eloquently, and, as it proved, successfully, for the passage of the bill.

But when, in 1827, it was attempted, in a section of a proposed bankrupt law, to establish universally for the country a system of insolvency and transfer the jurisdiction to the Court of the United States, Van Buren opposed it.

" The ninety-third section of this bill," he said, "is upon any definition that may be given of the different terms, an insolvent law. If Congress has the constitutional power to pass it, the States have no right to pass any law upon the subject of insolvency; not even to authorize the discharge of imprisoned debtors upon a process issuing out of their own courts, otherwise than as it may suit the pleasure or convenience of Congress to permit. There is no middle

ground. If the partition wall between bankruptcy and insolvency is once broken down,
all State legislation will be subjected to the
absolute and arbitrary supervision of Congress. I do not believe that such was the
design of the framers of the Constitution;
I do not believe that such is the Constitution; I therefore object to the constitutional power of Congress to pass the section
referred to. In my judgment, the provision contained in the ninety-third section
is not within the reasons which induced
the framers of the Constitution to vest in
Congress this power of establishing uniform
laws on the subject of bankruptcies; it is a
power which never ought to have been or
to be vested in Congress; it can only be
well and successfully executed by the States,
where those who made the Constitution
have left it; its exercise would operate most
injuriously upon the system which governs
the Union and the States separately. Those
mischiefs will, among other things, consist

in an injurious extension of the patronage
of the Federal Government, and an insup-
portable enlargement of the range of its
judicial power."

The same view of the duties of the General Government, with regard to foreign
powers, dictated the opposition of Van Buren to the design of sending envoys to the
Congress of American Nations, invited by
Bolivar to assemble at Panama. " Would
it be wise in us," he demanded, vainly opposing the nomination of a minister from
the United States to that body, "would it
be wise in us to change our established policy upon the subject of political connections with foreign States ?" With an accurate knowledge of the state of the question
and the warnings to be derived from our
own experience, he discussed the general
principle of avoiding all entangling alliances
on which our country stands alone among
the nations; and he argued that the condition of the Spanish-American States was

such as not to exempt them from the application of the rule.

" I yield to no man," said he, " in my anxious wishes for the success of the Spanish-American States. I will go as far as I think any American citizen ought to go to secure to them the blessings of free government. I commend the solicitude which has been manifested by our Government upon this subject, and have, of course, no desire to discourage it. But I am against all alliances, against all armed confederacies, or confederacies of any sort; come in what shape they may, I care not how specious or how disguised, I oppose them. The States in question have the power and the means, if united and true to their principles, to resist any force that Europe can send against them. It is only by being recreant to the principles upon which their revolution is founded, by suffering foreign influence to distract and divide them, that their independence can be endangered. But, happen what may, our course should be left to our choice, whenever occasion for acting shall occur.

" We require neither alliance nor agreement to compel us to perform whatever our duty enjoins. Our national character is our best and should be our only pledge. Meanwhile, let us bestow upon our neighbors, the young republics of the South, the moral aid of a good example. To make that example more salutary, let it exhibit our moderation in success, our firmness in adversity, our devotion to our country and its institutions, and, above all, that *sine qua non* to the existence of our republican government—our fidelity to a written Constitution. ' The moral aid of a good example' —that is the proper manner in which our republic is to exercise its influence on the world. America practises the lessons of freedom and inculcates them by her example. She has not the eager haste of that fanatical and ill-grounded conviction which

cannot rest satisfied without proselytes.
She knows that humanity is all bound together as one; and waits willingly for the
mysterious but certain influence, by which a
truth that has become the property of the
human mind, radiating in every direction,
gradually and certainly becomes the property of the whole race. Let her career be
such that the nations of the earth will look
to her as a guide. To an eager and active
philanthropy the rule may seem marked
with coldness and restraint; yet it is the
only one which will win the friendship of
the world, and calmly insinuate the principles of popular reform into the affections
of the whole family of man, and into the
governments of the earth."

The same rule swayed Van Buren in his
judgment on questions of a purely domestic character. The subject of slavery had
not forced its way into the councils of the
nation till after Van Buren retired from
the Senate. Yet, when a knowledge of his

opinion on the subject of any attempt on the part of the people of the North, through the exercise of political powers or political interests, to affect the relation of master and slave was desired, he adhered to the strict instruction of the fundamental law, and avowed with the utmost frankness that "without a change in the Constitution he did not see in what authority the General Government could interfere, even at the instance of either or of all the slave-holding States."

The spirit of a generous philanthropy is not always cautious in its efforts. Eagerly bent on achieving good, it is sometimes tempted to overstep the boundaries of law, and sometimes to make ravages in the defence of liberty. The assertion of the freedom of the seas was, from the formation of our Government, so mingled with our institutions that it cannot be abandoned without a wound upon the very life of our liberties. The slave-trade, against which, in a greater or less degree, Virginia had for a century protested, was justly the object of American reprobation. America took the lead in reprobating the traffic, and by her laws made it piracy. The eagerness of philanthropy now proposes that all the world should, as it were, be invited to join in executing our municipal law, and, as a consequence, should give to the assumption of the power to search a new and unheard-of latitude.

"From 1794 to 1808," said Van Buren, in the course of the debate on the Panama mission, "when the constitutional inhibition upon Congress in relation to the slave-trade expired, a system of wise and, as far as the power of the Government extended, efficient legislation was adopted for the suppression of that detestable traffic. From the latter period to the year 1819 our legislation assumed a wider range and a still more efficient character, until finally the offence was denounced as piracy, the punishment due to that crime prescribed, and the Executive clothed with power and means fully adequate to the execution of the law and the suppression of the trade, so far, at least, as our commerce is concerned. The measures then adopted effected the purpose for which they were designed. They did more : they extorted from England, who, next to the United States, has recently been foremost in the adoption of means to this end, the unqualified admission, not only that the United States had been the first, but also the most successful laborers in the cause of humanity."

To these measures Van Buren gave his hearty approbation. But as to any stipulation with England, "yielding, under certain modifications, the right of search, and authorizing a foreign power to enforce our own laws upon our own citizens," he gave a warning against it as "ill-advised," and having necessarily for "its results contention at home and dissatisfaction abroad."

He opposed every attempt to surrender the "control of our conduct in the support of our rights, or the discharge of our duties to foreign associations."

The people of the whole Union are wiser than the people of any individual State, for it includes the intelligence of that State with the wisdom of all the rest. The advancement of a senator of New York to a foremost place among the Democratic senators of the Union had an influence in eliminating errors in the opinion of the Democracy of New York. In the course of the year, 1827, this became apparent.

The industry of the country was advancing with such rapidity that the country gazed with astonishment at the immense production of its own labor, and all voices united to cheer the enterprise and industry of our people. Men forgot that they prospered under the genial influences of institutions which gave a free career to activity, and stimulated the vigorous mind in the workshop to unfold all its inventive powers. They longed to hasten the development of industry by protection.

This feeling was strengthened by political recollections. The promotion of American manufactures had in their infancy been the test of patriotism. The desire of a common regulation of commerce had assisted to form the Union. The necessity of enforcing neutral rights had hastened the development of American manufactures. The embargo, the interruption of commerce with Great Britain, had compelled their increase; the war raised a demand for the domestic manufacture of all that was necessary for national defence. The war, too, occasioned a debt which required a large revenue for its discharge. Hence American statesmen, after the war, joined to promote the mining of iron, the growth of cotton and of wool, and the manufacture of them all, by heavy duties on their importation from abroad.

In 1824 Van Buren, in obedience to the

10

known wishes of his constituents, gave a silent vote for the tariff of that year; but political aspirants of all parts of the country became aware of the rising zeal for fostering its own productions, and sought to avail themselves of the generous and deeply seated regard for the industry of America in its competition with Great Britain.

Van Buren was one of the first to perceive that the great interests of America were thus to be jeoparded by the eager selfishness of ambitious politicians; and when, in 1827, the country was convulsed with the effort to excite a universal ferment, and by means of it to win the way to political power, Van Buren, whose "personal feelings," as I have been informed by one of his most intimate friends, "have been at all times adverse to the high tariff policy," calmly and temperately opposed the movement. At a moment when all New York seemed carried away with a passionate desire to foster the nation's industry by national legislation, when his warm friends wavered, and a current was setting against the more liberal views, Van Buren repaired to Albany, and by his healing counsels restored confidence and harmony.* This was one of the moments of his life where his self-possession was most commanding. He appeared among those who had been led to believe a doubt on the subject of a high tariff to be fatal; and almost, as it were, the first eminent member of Congress from the north of the Potomac, in July, 1827, he pointed to the danger of subjecting the industry of the country to the fluctuations of party success, and gave his warning against "a measure proceeding more from the closet of the politician than from the workshop of the manufacturer." His argument was addressed

---

* These facts of Van Buren's appearance and speech at Albany, and the great effect that his self-possession and calmness had over the Democratic party, which, till he came, was yielding to despondency, were given me by Governor Marcy.

to the agriculturalist of the country, as the safe umpire in the dispute.

His own intrepidity preserved the confidence and cheered the spirits of his friends; it could not at once break down wrong maxims in political economy, which the majority of the country had in some measure connected with the pride of nationality. But this was the moment when the flood of opinion at the North in favor of a high tariff received a check.

The elections of 1827 passed over, and the Democracy of New York, and generally of the other States, had triumphed. Every omen promised the approaching success of the Democratic party in the Union. Van Buren had been re-elected to the American Senate by a great majority; and when, in December, he repaired to Washington to enter on his second period of service, his own honorable fame gave assurances that new scenes of activity would open before him. He began the winter's career, his last as a senator, with renewed vigor and brilliancy. A tardy justice had not yet made provision for the declining years of the officers of the Revolution. A distrust of a system of pensions and other causes united to make the provision for them doubtful. The bill reported for that end seemed to many on the point of being lost. In January, 1828, just as the discussion was coming to an end, Van Buren rose for its support, and throwing his heart into his theme, without premeditation, spoke generous words with persuasive power. A new and more favorable complexion was put upon the subject by his speech, which led to a compromise of conflicting opinions and the passage of the bill in a modified form.

During the busy activity of the session, and the most earnest strife in the Senate on questions agitating the country, De Witt Clinton, then Governor of New York, in the height of his fame, suddenly expired at Albany. When the news of his death reached

Washington, the members from New York, without distinction of party, held a meeting to pay a tribute to his memory.

"The triumph of his talents and patriotism," said Van Buren, "cannot fail to become monuments of high and enduring fame. We cannot, indeed, but remember that in our public career collisions of opinion and action, at once extensive, earnest, and enduring, have arisen between the deceased and many of us. For myself, sir, it gives me a deep-felt satisfaction to know, and more so to be conscious that the deceased also felt and acknowledged, that our political differences have been wholly free from that most venomous and corroding of all poisons, personal hatred.

"But in other respects it is now immaterial what was the character of those collisions. They have been turned to nothing, and less than nothing, by the event we deplore; and I doubt not that we will, with one voice and one heart, yield to his mem-

ory the well-deserved tribute of our respect
for his name, and our warmest gratitude for
his great and signal services. For myself,
sir, so strong, so sincere, and so engrossing
is that feeling, that I, who, while living,
never, no, never, envied him anything, now
that he has fallen, am greatly tempted to
envy him his grave with its honors."

In the winter of 1828 a tariff bill reached
the Senate, of a character which the wisdom
of the country soon afterwards essentially
modified. Public opinion in New York
had not yet fully learned to respect that
freedom of trade which can furnish to our
looms wool from flocks that pasture at the
antipodes, and supply the inland provinces
of China with tea-chests from the mines of
Wisconsin. The Legislature of New York
took the subject into consideration, and,
with the concurrence of all parties in the
Legislature, by a unanimous vote on the
main question in the Senate, by a vote of
ninety-eight to three in the House, the sen-

ators of New York in Congress were in-
structed to vote for the bill. Van Buren,
holding obedience to instructions a cardinal
doctrine of Democracy, overcame his own
repugnance to the provisions of the tariff
act of 1828, and gave to it a reluctant assent, "in obedience," said Senator Benton,
"to a principle which we both hold sacred."
But Van Buren, whose career in Congress
was now to close, did not leave the Senate
without most decidedly expressing his own
views on the fountain of evil from which the
errors in our administration had sprung.

A resolution had been proposed in the
Senate, tending to attribute to the Vice-
President by inference and independent of
established rules, an 'inherent, irresponsible
power to restrain debate. How dangerous
such a power would be, in the hands of an
officer not elected by the Senate, and not
responsible to it, is apparent; but beyond
that lay the fact that such a construction
of the Constitution would change the char-

acter of the Union. Van Buren regarded this question as one of the forms under which the difference of parties may be stated. The party of the past desire governments like those of the past, centralized, and having authority; the party of the future look to the boundless expanse of our country, and labor to build up a system of constitutional law suited to an ever-increasing land. Van Buren arose to defend that construction of the Constitution which should least interfere with the appropriate action of the States and with the freedom of individual industry; and he spoke on the collision between the rights of the few and the many —those never-ceasing conflicts between the advocates of the enlargement and concentration of power on the one hand, and its limitation and distribution on the other. " The division of the country into the two great political parties is mainly to be ascribed," said Van Buren, "to the struggle between the two great opposing principles which have been in active operation in this country from the closing scenes of the Revolutionary War to the present day." " The former," he argued, "has grown out of a deep and settled distrust of the people and of the States; the antagonistic principle has its origin in a jealousy of power, justified by all human experience." He insisted that from the moment of the adoption of the Constitution, "the advocates of a strong government had been at work to obtain, by construction, what was not intended to be included in the grant;" and as a senator from New York, the foremost commercial State in the Union, he took part in forming an organized opposition to the system of centralization.

The incorporation of the Bank of the United States he denounced as " the great pioneer of constitutional encroachments." " By the civil revolution of 1800," he further said, "the public sentiment was improved, our public councils purified, the spirit of encroachment severely rebuked, and, it was then hoped, extinguished forever. During Jefferson's administration, and with a single exception, that of Madison, the Government was administered upon the principles which the framers of the Constitution avowed, and which their constituents had ratified, and the people once and again had confirmed. After a hard struggle the charter of the Bank of the United States was suffered to expire; and the conceded and well-understood powers of the Government were found amply sufficient to enable it to perform the great functions for which it was instituted. During a large portion of the time, the country was blessed with a degree of prosperity and happiness without a parallel in the world. At the close of Madison's administration, a new bank was incorporated, and received his reluctant assent. It will be shutting our eyes to the truth to deny, or attempt to conceal the fact, that that assent, coming from the quarter that it did, has had

a most powerful and far from salutary influence on the subsequent course of the Government. Its author had himself, on a former occasion, demonstrated the want of
power in the Federal Government to in-
corporate a bank; and his assent was now
placed on the express ground, that the recognition of the authority of the Government
in relation to the old bank by the State
governments and the courts as well as the
people, had precluded the question of its
constitutionality. In this way the power in
question had become a successful interpo-
lation upon the text of the Constitution.

"The time," he continued, "is not far distant when the interpolations which have
been made on the Constitution, with the
sophisms by which they were supported,
will be subjects of severe reprehension."

He roused public attention against the
Bank of the United States. With all the
weight to be derived from his position, as
the chosen leader of the Democracy of New

York, with the confidence of the Democracy of the Union, soon to be named Governor of his native State, and designated by universal opinion for the highest place in the Cabinet if Democracy in the nation should be successful, Van Buren invited the country to an issue against the institution, which in his opinion had been an abundant source of corrupting influences, and "the pioneer of encroachment on the Constitution."

New York, by the hand of George Clinton, gave the casting vote against renewing the old Bank of the United States; New York, by the voice of Van Buren, opposed the continuance of its successor, and made it the dividing question in the conflict of parties.

CHAPTER V.

VAN BUREN AS SECRETARY OF STATE, AS MIN-
ISTER, AND AS VICE-PRESIDENT: 1829–1837.

VAN BUREN retired from the Senate of
the United States, after serving in that body
for more than seven years. His uniform
courtesy of manner disarmed political hatred
of its bitterness; and his private life was
marked by the decorum and purity which
leave no occasion for concealments, apolo-
gies, or denials. The discussions in which
he engaged called the nation to active inquiry, and the spirit of party was summoned
on the one side and on the other to plead
before the high tribunal of the people.

Meanwhile the calm circumspection and
the union which marked the movements of
the Democracy of New York, conciliated for
it the confidence of that State. In the au-

tumn of 1828, on the eve of the Presidential election, Van Buren, by the acclamation of his party, was named its candidate
for governor. He was opposed by Smith
Thompson, one of the judges of the Supreme Court of the United States, a statesman and lawyer known throughout the
Union, of an eminence which made him a
worthy antagonist. In the midst of highest
excitement, a majority of the districts gave
their vote for Jackson; the Legislature was
in both branches most decidedly Democratic.
Van Buren received about thirty thousand
votes more than his opponent, and by this
vast plurality was, on the first day of January, 1829, borne to the highest office in the
gift of the people of New York.

In the few weeks of his service as the
chief magistrate of a commonwealth first
in commerce, in internal improvements, in
wealth, in numbers, in freedom of fran-
chises, and in boundless promises from fu-
turity, he distinguished himself by provi-

dent care for the people and by hatred of monopoly.

In New York, sales at auction of imported goods had been restricted to officers appointed by the Government; in his message to the Legislature, Van Buren rebuked the monopoly, and it was abolished.

He proposed stringent enactments to prevent the use of money in elections, and to leave elections free to the unbiassed action of the popular mind.

Another important and humane measure was the establishment of the Safety Fund. Millions of bank-notes were constantly in circulation without adequate means for their redemption ; and the unwary, and those least connected with banks, those who were in no manner benefited by banks, were the most exposed to suffer loss.

Who, that has not seen, can describe the anguish of the emigrant of those days when, arriving at the land-office, he found the banknotes in which he had hoarded the fruits of a life of toil, or the modest proceeds of his patrimony, had suddenly lost their value before the end of his journey? Who can recount the misery and widely spread woe at the farmer's fireside as he finds the fruit of all his toil, exchanged for bank-notes, melting away from him through the mischiefs of a depreciating currency? Many a heart-rending scene has been witnessed in the years that are but recently gone by, when fraudulent issues of paper have held the bitter cup of poverty to the lips of families whose industry and frugality entitled them to competence. And these issues of paper were authorized by State Legislatures; so that the frauds seemed to have arrayed themselves in the reflected character of public obligations.

The evils of our banking system, more overwhelmingly apparent in the disastrous reverses at the great centres of commercial business, carried untold sorrow to the abodes of humble industry. Van Buren was aware

11

of the cruel wrongs from which the less
wealthy, the soberly industrious, were suffering; he saw and avowed that it was as yet
beyond his power to remedy the evil in its
source; but at least care might be taken
that the laborer and the farmer and those
who are ignorant of the ways of banks
should be protected against loss from corporations which the Legislature of the State
lent its authority to establish. To that end
he resolved on raising a reserved fund for
the security of holders of notes issued by
the banks of New York. To the banks,
which, from their daily business, well knew
the condition, character, and solvency of
each other, power was given, through commissioners and the Chancery Court, season-
ably to enjoin any bank, and arrest its issues; and, to protect the community fully,
a fund, raised by a tax of one-half per cent.
on all banks included within the law, was
set apart for the immediate redemption of
the bills in circulation, issued by a bank

which should be thus forced into liquidation. In this way the notes of banks in the State of New York were never to become a loss to the holder; and although the improvidence of legislation still permitted the fluctuations incident to the use of paper for money, a guarantee was at least secured that the laborer should not be cursed with a worthless currency. The plan, for a season at least, accomplished that end. It was proposed only as a dike to protect holders of notes against rashness and frauds which directors of banks could foresee, but which most men could learn only after their consummation.

On the 4th of March, 1829, Andrew Jackson was inaugurated as President of the United States; and he immediately summoned Van Buren to take the highest station in his Cabinet. Amid the applause of his friends and with the express approbation of the Legislature of his own State, which was proud of his advancement, he resigned the post of Governor of New York, and entered into the service of the United States as the counsellor of Jackson in conducting the foreign relations of his country. He repaired to Washington with the full and affectionate confidence of the Democracy of his native State, and the best hopes of the Democracy of the country. " I called him to the Department of State," said Andrew Jackson, "influenced by the general wish and expectation of the Republican party throughout the Union."

His position in the Cabinet was peculiar. No one of the other members of the administration had ever before occupied a similar executive post; but of Van Buren the school of preparation had been a long career of service in the Senate, and the President reposed in him special confidence, not from personal and political friendship only, but from trust in his practical judgment and experience.

Placed in a position that gave him oppor-

tunity of counsel in the distribution of patronage, it may surprise the incredulous to
learn that he always refused to incline its
exercise to the furtherance of his own ul-
terior advancement; and his nearest personal friends, in like manner, refused every
request to bias the appointing power, being
resolved to support the administration of
Jackson with single-minded fidelity. For
long years Van Buren, in the Senate, had
struggled, against an obstinate majority, to
define the just principles of the construction
of the Constitution. When summoned to
give counsel in the Cabinet on the Maysville veto, he had the pleasure of seeing
the exact views he had urged as a senator
enforced by the Executive, and made the
property of the country by the decision of
Andrew Jackson. How do our institutions
effect the education of the people! Debates had assisted to develop just views of
national policy; and now, by the appropriate exercise of the grand tribunitial power

with which the President is invested, those views reached every home, knocked for entrance at every heart, and summoned every citizen in the Union to give deliberate judgment between the legislative branches of the Government and the President. "You will ruin your party and your own prospects," they said to the old hero. "Providence," answered Andrew Jackson, "will take care of me." Nothing could turn aside his resolve to exercise the veto, and never, in the end, was a public act more universally approved.

The conspicuous subject in our foreign relations was the interruption of direct commerce with the British colonies. This interruption was most deeply involved in that restrictive system which European nations, in their system of colonization, rigorously adopted. America, while dependent, had keenly felt the injustice of admitting England to all its ports and all its territories, and being restricted in its commerce with a large part of the British dominions.

From the first moment of conversation
with Franklin for peace, this discrepancy
had been pointed out; and the justice of
genuine reciprocity in intercourse between
all American territory and all the possessions of Great Britain had been maintained.
It was certain that it would one day be
maintained successfully. The administration of 1824 at first formally made the demand, but withdrew it, thinking correctly
that the time for it was not come. Great
Britain offered a conditional liberty of traffic
with her colonies, if accepted within a limited
period. The period expired without a communication from America. Afterwards, the
administration of Quincy Adams proposed
to accept the conditional right of traffic,
but Great Britain haughtily refused the
renewal of the offer of what she pretended to consider "a boon." He that will
gain a view of the question, without reference to party, should read Van Buren's
speech, in which he urged upon Congress

to strengthen the arm of the administration by energetically arraying its whole influence on the side of our Government.

" Conflicting opinions," he had said,
" should be confined to subjects which
concern ourselves.   In the collisions which
may arise between the United States and a
foreign power, it is our duty to present an
unbroken front ; domestic differences, if
they tend to give encouragement to unjust
pretensions, should be extinguished or de-
ferred ; and the cause of our Government
must be considered as the cause of our
country. . . .

" Our acts should be firm, and, however
mild and conciliatory, should exhibit neither
fickleness nor irresolution. If, retracing
our steps, we abandon the principle which
alone prevented an amicable adjustment
in 1824, the act announcing the fact should
also proclaim our unalterable determination,
should our views not be met in a conciliatory spirit, to accept of nothing less than

that which justice demands. We have to contend with an adversary deeply versed in the arts of diplomacy, and every way competent to discern the intentions of those whose interests may come in competition with their own. By deferring the operation of the act until Congress again meet, you will awaken some doubt of your ultimate intention, and perhaps a hope may arise that you are not now prepared to renounce a trade in which you are not permitted to participate on equitable terms. With such an alternative before us, there is no one in this Senate—I trust there is no one in this nation—who would hesitate one moment in his choice. In giving utterance to this universal sentiment, let your act be explicit and your determination final. Leave nothing to be accomplished by a future Congress; and, in the act which you may pass, present to the British Government your ultimatum, in the terms which she has herself proposed. In this there will neither be menace nor an offensive display. It is precisely the course which she pursued when the situation of parties was reversed. If it be the intention of Great Britain to place this trade upon the footing of just reciprocity, she will not be moved from her purpose by mere questions of form; but if, influenced by any change in her views or policy, she is resolved to reject our liberal propositions, no phraseology, however courteous, will produce a different determination. Be this determination what it may, we shall have performed our duty, and may rely upon the support of the American people."

In conducting the foreign relations of the country, Van Buren carried these views into effect. England refused to abide by the terms which she first offered, because the former American administration had delayed to accept her proposition within a stipulated time. Two successive ministers had, by the previous administration, solicited the liberties once offered, but had so-

licited them in vain. Van Buren saw the
necessity of making the subject a national
question. He insisted that the misunder-
standing which had arisen must be transient; that if Great Britain persevered in
withholding what she had offered, it must
be considered as an offence to the whole
country.

This representation was successful; and
the colonial question, which had baffled the
country for several years, and of which the
settlement had been vainly attempted by
Gallatin and by Barbour, was promptly settled on the terms which the previous administration had sought from Great Britain.

Other negotiations were conducted with
equal success. The election of Andrew
Jackson had produced a strong effect on
the civilized world. The European nations,
weary of the ancient formal round of diplomacy, saw with delight an energetic statesman at the head of the American Government. As Secretary of State, Van Buren

seized the opportunity with promptness and untiring diligence.

The treaty for indemnity was begun with France; Denmark adjusted the demands of American citizens; Spain made compensation for her wrong-doings, and relaxed her restrictive regulations to our advantage; Portugal gave indemnity; Austria and Turkey were brought into commercial relations with the young republic of the west. With Russia an opening was made for similar agreements. In America the relations with Mexico and with Colombia were relieved of embarrassments. The two years of Van Buren's service as Secretary of State were distinguished by his effective industry.

His position could not be contemplated without envy. Divisions entered the Cabinet. Van Buren, who, as secretary, had steadfastly, pursued the good of the country, and had on all occasions forborne by the influence of patronage to advance his personal pretensions, now formed the honorable design of securing tranquillity to the administration of General Jackson by retiring from his post, and in June, 1831, resigned his office. The President, justly esteeming his fidelity and experience, named him Minister to Great Britain. His political friends, who hoped to see him one day elevated to the Presidency, urged him not to accept the appointment. They warned him against withdrawing himself from his country at such a moment; how entirely he would be removed from the immediate eye of his countrymen; how certainly his absence, though in the public service, would delay or prevent his advancement in popular affection at home. But Van Buren had always separated himself from intrigue, and wished to be separated from even the appearance of it; and in honorable self-reliance accepting the appointment, he, in August, 1831, repaired to Great Britain. From his long career in the Senate and in the Cabinet, he was thoroughly acquainted with the state of our relations with Great Britain. No man more enjoyed the confidence of the President and of the country. Every omen promised auspicious results from his mission.

His political friends had entreated Van Buren not to accept this appointment. They had held up to him the ill influence his absence from the country might exercise on his future advancement; that public service abroad would remove him from the immediate eye of the people. What his friends vainly desired to accomplish, his enemies achieved.

Against a man who had been for twenty years in public life—whose private integrity, purity of life, and political consistency were unimpeachable—it was difficult to find cause of censure. They charged him with intrigue; but, keeping far aloof from the strifes of connections and factions and parties, he had voluntarily left the country.

The ground finally assigned for the re-

jection of Van Buren as Minister to Great
Britain was found in an instruction to Mc-
Lane, which Andrew Jackson claimed to
have dictated. Van Buren had said in the
Senate that the strife with England must
be, on the part of the United States, a national one, not interfered with by any local
party strife. The ministry of Great Britain,
having taken back the offer made to a
former administration to open her West In-
dia ports to the United States because that
administration had neglected a compliance
with a form, was now summoned to continue
her offer, or to place her refusal on some
other ground than the acts of the late administration; and clothing remonstrance in
the mildest form, Van Buren added that
otherwise the ministry of Great Britain
"would not fail to excite the deepest sensi-
bility of the people."

His words were perverted, as though he
invited England to be a party to our strifes
—he who had summoned the whole country

to a united expression of opinion and united assertion of American rights. A majority of the Senate, assuming that their instructions were an invitation to European governments to participate in our domestic strifes, rejected his nomination by a party vote, and thus compelled the diplomacy of all Europe to watch the verdict of the American people on this vote of an accidental majority of their Senate.

From the people of the Union there rose a general murmur of disapprobation. The Legislature of New York unanimously addressed a letter to the President of the United States, bearing testimony to the high respect of their State for the personal and public merit of its proscribed statesman; the Democracy of the Union immediately placed him in nomination for the Vice-presidency; and the people, by the vote of two hundred and eighty-six electors against one hundred and eighty-nine, elected him to preside over the body which had re-

jected him. The speech with which he entered on his official duties won universal
applause for its propriety and dignity. The
Senate, at a later day, by a unanimous vote,
made a declaration "of the impartiality, dignity, and ability with which he presided
over their deliberations, and of their entire
approbation of his conduct as President of
the Senate."

Elevated to the second highest office in
our land, his sympathies remained, as they
had ever been, with the class from which he
had sprung and by which he had been elevated—the more numerous and less wealthy.
In May, 1833, the unenfranchised mechanics of Rhode Island addressed him to obtain
his mature opinion on the subject of general
suffrage, and he did not hesitate to lend all
the weight of his station and of his judgment, enlightened and confirmed as it had
been by experience in his own State, in
favor of enfranchising the mechanic and the
laborer. He modestly recapitulated the his-

12

tory of the settlement of the franchise in New York. " In acting upon this subject," he added, " my own course has never been influenced by any apprehension that it would be dangerous to the rights of property to extend the right of voting to those who were without property. Our experience has, I think, fully demonstrated that in a community like that which composes a great majority in every State in our confederacy, there is no reason for alarm in this respect.

"At an earlier period of my public life I was not entirely free from apprehensions of the influence of wealth upon so extended a suffrage as that which is now possessed in New York. Upon this head, however, we are now able to speak from full and satisfactory experience. It has given me the highest gratification to be convinced that my fears were without adequate foundation."

As Vice-president, Van Buren was at the side of Jackson during his second term as

President. It was the period of the first experiment in producing panics; of reckless
expansions of the currency; of extravagant
speculation; of an accumulating surplus revenue; of the last struggles of the Bank of
the United States for the continuance of its
powers. There was not a difficult question
on which Jackson did not open his mind to
the Vice-president with complete and affectionate confidence. He has often been heard
to narrate incidents illustrating the prompt
decision and bold judgment of his younger
friend; and in those days of vehement conflicts between the power of the people and
interests embodied against that power, the
daring energy of the one was well united
with the more tranquil intrepidity of the
other.

How fully this was recognized by the
people appears from the action of the Democratic party of the Union. In May, 1835,
it assembled in convention at Baltimore,
and by a unanimous vote placed Van Bu-

ren in nomination as their candidate for the Presidency.

His opponents, whose fears gave assurances of his rapid advancement, had never ceased to calumniate him as an adept in management and intrigue. The hearty unanimity of the convention refuted the suggestion; for intrigue and management always generate jealousy and division. To the official letter communicating his nomination, he sent a memorable reply.

" The nomination," he wrote, " you have been deputed to announce to me presents the only contingency upon the occurrence of which I could consent to become a candidate for the high office of President of the United States. When my name was first associated with the question of General Jackson's successor, more through the illwill of opponents than the partiality of friends, I determined to wait for the development of the views of the Republicans of the Union, and to pursue that course only which their unbiassed judgment should finally recommend. I deemed that course to be due to the administration of which I was a member, to the best interests of the country, and to the indivisibility of a political party, by the original organization of which the overthrow of republican principles in the United States was prevented, and upon the ascendency of which we can alone depend for their preservation. To the offers of support which were at that period occasionally made to me from different quarters of the Union, I respectfully replied that the public good required the services of General Jackson for a second term; that the agitation of the question of his successor, at that early period, must of necessity embarrass the administration; and that it was my desire that my name should not be connected with the subject. From that time to the present I have neither solicited the aid, nor sought the support, of any man in reference to the high office for which I have

been nominated (unless my replies to inter-
rogatories from my fellow-citizens upon public questions, and my sincere endeavors to
make myself worthy of the respect and confidence of the American people, are liable
to that construction). For the truth of this
declaration I can safely appeal to the hundreds of honorable men who composed the
recent convention ; to the numerous editors
and politicians throughout the Union who
have distinguished me by their preference ;
and to my private correspondents and intimate friends, not excepting the consid-
erable number of persons, once my friends
and associates, whom the fluctuations of
political life have converted into opponents. In none of these classes, or in any
other of our community, is there a man
who can truly say that I have solicited
his political support, or that I have entered,
or sought to enter, with him into any ar-
rangement to bring about the nomination
which I have now received, or to secure

my elevation to the Chief Magistracy of my country.

"The liberal men of all parties, I trust, and you and those you represent, I am sure will pardon me for having thus spoken of my own conduct in reference to a point upon which I have been the silent object of attack, as causeless as it has been violent and unremitted; especially as I alone can answer for it in relation to all my country-men, although thousands may be ready to answer in relation to themselves."

It should be added that not the violence of party spirit, not the perversion of malice, not the voice of calumny, ever insinuated in any one instance a denial of this unquali-fied assertion; nor have the years which followed, the events of which changed so many who had once been Van Buren's friends into implacable opponents, called forth a single individual to question the ex-act accuracy of his statement. Those who knew him most intimately have made known

how remote were his character and habits
of thought and action from management,
intrigue, or concealment.

Yet at this period of his life there were
not wanting those who mistook his moderation for want of frankness, and, on public
questions of deepest interest, believed him
secret and uncommunicative. In a long career in the Senate, where he never shunned
taking part in the discussion of any question, his opinions had been avowed in debate, and by his votes made a matter of
record in the public journals. His life had
been a struggle against the enemies of popular power; he had ever been ready to repel their aggressions, yet without sharing
their passions. Once, in the spring of 1826,
at a moment when, in the Senate Chamber
in Washington, Van Buren was earnestly
engaged in the most hearty and open conflict with the friends of John Quincy Adams
and Henry Clay, the *Argus*, an able and
cautious Democratic journal at Albany, for

a time and solely from local causes, proposed
"to let the national politics alone." The
silence of the editor was attributed to the
influence of Van Buren; but accident has
placed within my reach the certain evidence
that the course which was then for a very
short period deliberately adopted, was adopted without his knowledge and to his surprise. For himself, he had not disguised
his preferences, yet the impression remained,
and many, mistaking the good-temper and
careful precision with which he had expressed himself for want of vigor, believed, or
pretended to believe, that he kept himself
uncommitted on public questions. Deceived
by this prejudice, in April, 1836, Sherrod
Williams, of Kentucky, a member of Congress, a vehement political opponent of Van
Buren, and a friend of Henry Clay, was put
forward to play the part of an inquisitor.
"I done so in good faith," wrote Sherrod
Williams, as if in reply to those who smiled
at his indecorum; and he again asked for

the views of the Democratic "candidate" for the Presidency, on topics like that of distributing portions of the national revenue, and of chartering a national bank. Van Buren seized the occasion of reaffirming his well-known opinions, and thus replied:

"It is my firm conviction that any system by which a distribution is made among the States, of moneys collected by the Federal Government, would introduce vices into the legislation of both governments, productive of the most injurious effects, as well upon the best interests of the country as upon the perpetuity of our political institutions. . . .

"It is now for the majority of the people to decide whether the distribution of the public deposits shall be the parent and forerunner of future distributions of the public revenue. I hope and believe that the public voice will demand that this species of legislation shall terminate with the emergency that produced it. . . .

" The public of the United States have a greater interest in an early settlement and substantial improvement of the public lands than in the amount of revenue which may be derived from them. . . .

" I am of the opinion that the avails of the public lands will be more equitably and faithfully applied ' to the common benefit of the United States,' by their continued appli- cation to the general wants of the Treasury, than by any other mode that has yet been suggested; and that such an appropriation is in every respect preferable to the distribu- tion thereof among the States. Entertain- ing these views, I cannot give you any encouragement that I will, in the event of my election to the Presidency, favor that policy. . . . My opposition to the establish- ment of a United States Bank in any of the States is placed on the want of constitu- tional power in Congress to establish one; and I am not only willing, but desirous, that the people of the United States should be

fully informed of the precise ground I occupy upon this subject. I desire more especially that they should know it now, when
an opportunity, the best our form of government affords, will soon be presented to express their opinion of its propriety. If they
are in favor of a national bank as a permanent branch of their institutions, or if they
desire a chief magistrate who will consider
it his duty to watch the course of events,
and give or withhold his assent to such an
institution according to the degree of necessity for it that may in his opinion arise from
the considerations to which your question
refers, they will see that my co-operation in
the promotion of either of these views cannot be expected. If, on the other hand,
with this seasonable, explicit, and published
avowal before them, a majority of the people of the United States shall, nevertheless,
bestow upon me their suffrages for the office of President, scepticism itself must cease
to doubt, and admit their will to be, that

there shall not be any Bank of the United States until the people, in the exercise of their sovereign authority, see fit to give to Congress the right to establish one. . . .

" Even if there was not a single bank, State or national, in the country, it would nevertheless be quite easy to place its domestic exchanges upon an advantageous and safe footing, so long as there is a sufficiency of solid capital to be employed in the business. From the nature of the thing itself, and from the experience of Europe, we may be assured that the profits and necessities of trade would invite and obtain ample facilities for the business of exchange from other sources, so long as the commercial community with one accord desire to see it successfully carried on, and assist in good faith in effecting it. . . .

" Gold and silver should constitute a much greater proportion of the circulating medium of the country than they now do. To protect the working-classes (who, generally speaking, have no control over a paper currency, and derive no profit from bank stock) against losses arising from depreciation, by securing a metallic currency sufficient at least for all minor dealings—including the payment of labor, the most important as well as the most pressing use there is for money—to furnish a more substantial specie basis for that part of the currency which consists of paper, and thereby save the whole community from loss in consequence of any sudden withdrawal of confidence—should be our 'first object,' as it is our imperative duty. . . .

" There are, in my opinion, objections to the re-establishment of a national bank, of a character not inferior to any that I have stated.   The supremacy of the popular will is the foundation of our government."

The Democracy of the Union supported Van Buren with entire unanimity. . Out of two hundred and eighty-six electoral votes he received one hundred and seventy; and, for the first time, the Democracy of the North saw itself represented in the Presidential chair. Electoral votes were given for Van Buren without regard to geographical divisions: New York and Alabama, Missouri and Maine, Virginia and Connecticut, were found standing together. His election seemed friendly to the harmony and the perpetuity of the Union.

CHAPTER VI.

VAN BUREN AS PRESIDENT OF THE UNITED STATES: MARCH 4, 1837—MARCH 4, 1841.

On the 4th of March, 1837, Van Buren took the oath of office as President of the United States, to which station he had been raised by the Democratic party of America. For the country he invoked days of pleasantness and paths of peace; but during his administration he was called to a more severe struggle in behalf of popular power than the legislative history of the country had ever known.

For eight years Van Buren had, within his own State of New York, possessed the support of the Democracy, and general suffrage was introduced.

For nearly eight years he defended in the Senate the strict construction of the Constitution.

For eight years more he had co-operated with Andrew Jackson in his devotedness to the same cause, which now found support in the Executive. But as in mechanics opposing forces produce sideway motions, so, in the immense collision between the popular judgment and the moneyed interest, the decision, though a victory for the people, sometimes resulted in a measure that was not in itself the adequate expression of the intended policy of the administration. Thus, in the struggle with the United States Bank, there still remained in the expedient of deposit banks something of the same perverse influence and interest, though no longer united in a single gigantic corporation. In like manner, the struggle against internal improvements by the National Government, and the accumulating revenue consequent on the complete payment of the national debt, led both branches of Congress to distribute among the States the proceeds of the public lands, and afterwards to de-

13

posit with them the accumulating excess of national revenue.

The career of speculation had led to vast purchases of public lands by moneys which were borrowed of the deposit banks and expended at the land-offices. These sums the land-offices promptly redeposited in the banks from which they had been momentarily withdrawn, and were loaned out again as fast as they were received, to be again employed in the same purposes of speculation by the acquisition of public lands. Andrew Jackson, then President of the United States, rightly doubting the solvency of some of the deposit banks, by a circular letter emanating from the executive branch of the Government, commanded the price of public lands to be paid in specie, the only legal tender of the Constitution, but without any preparatory act of Congress which as yet had refused to share his distrust. The Treasury order, therefore, which might have been a wholesome check and admonition, served for the moment to irritate and increase the excitement.

This was the condition of the country when Van Buren, who had no halo of mili tary glory or Revolutionary service to conciliate popularity, was called upon to stand out against the beneficiaries of bank-paper, organized as a political party.

This movement in the world of industry led, from two causes, towards a diminution of prices. Long years of nearly universal peace had increased the productive power. In the price of nearly every great article of production there was a marked tendency to a decline, resulting also from another fact — that the business to be transacted increased faster than the supplies of gold and silver, which were the measures of value.

To check the action of these two causes there had been a general resort to the use of credit, till its expansion became out of proportion to its resources. In commerce,

as elsewhere, general laws ultimately prevailed, and the result was inevitable.

In America, where prices had attained an
unnatural elevation, this unavoidable result
of a diminution of prices was heightened by
an accumulation of reverses, all tending to
a sudden explosion at the very period when
Van Buren began to administer the government.

In addition to the long-continued efforts
of the business world to maintain high
prices came the peculiar fact that the Bank
of the United States, for the purpose of producing the greatest political effect and ex-
torting new powers from the country, had
expanded its discounts, and that the hundreds of State banks had followed its example. The spirit of speculation grew wild,
and, excited by the increasing opulence and
numbers of the country, pursued its game
with an unreasoning determination to real-
ize at once the profits that could only spring
from the industry of future millions. The

delusion grew to an astonishing height, nursed by the immense increase of the population, by the wild hopes of inflamed imaginations, and by an inflated currency.

The increase of the circulation had expanded prices, and, as a consequence, promoted enormous importations of foreign goods, and creating a balance against us to foreigners of thirty to sixty millions of dollars.

While high prices were followed by an excess of importations, many State Legislatures, sharing in some measure a general impulse, had simultaneously incurred debts abroad for money to be lavished on internal improvements. The money thus raised in Europe was remitted by shipments of merchandise that were sold in the market at home.

Free institutions won confidence. Foreign capitalists loaned money readily to new States, whose industry as yet produced little for the foreign market but wheat.

England was willing to lend millions, while she excluded from her market the only product of the soil which could furnish means of payment. To individuals open credits were freely extended, and often without limitation as to time.

The crisis was at hand just as Van Buren entered on his administration, and its dangers and difficulties had been immensely increased by unwise legislation.

The high tariff, which hastened the payment of the national debt, raised too much revenue after the debt was discharged, and was only gradually reduced, the reduction proceeding too slowly, and extending ultimately too far. A large surplus revenue had accumulated, and this revenue, by an act of June, 1836, was to be deposited—so the act of distribution was called—among the States; and this surplus revenue, amounting to six-and-thirty millions, was in the process of distribution among the States at the moment of Van Buren's inauguration. This proved the most grievous and injurious act of the whole.

But the Congress which had nearly exhausted the Treasury by distribution did, also, in its second session, make most unusually large appropriations, the opponents of Van Buren demanding and advocating them with great unanimity.

Every financial evil at once gathered round the administration of Van Buren. The contraction of the banks, the depreciation of all kinds of property, the paralysis of business, cut off the public resources.

The effects of the revulsion were first visible in New York. Debts in Great Britain had been contracted beyond the ability of merchants to pay; large and unavailable credits had been extended to traders in the interior of the country. Men were more and more startled as, by degrees, the amount of indebtment to England became known. The moneys of the Government, according to the law of 1836, enacted under an anti-

Democratic bias, were, in the process of distribution, deranging, with convulsive energy, the whole system of the deposit banks. All joined to hurry the curtailment of the currency; prices fell far below their natural level. The tempest broke on the wise and the unwise, on the fraudulent and on the honest. The whole community was involved in the great disaster.

The merchants of New York, unwilling to confess over-trading; the speculators, refusing to condemn themselves for yielding to the bad counsels of eager cupidity; the laborers, on whose innocent heads the storm had burst, all sent their committees to the General Government for relief.

But what could the Government do? The revenue was collected by bonds, of which Congress might postpone the day of payment. The revenue of the country had, through the deposit banks, already been loaned. Holding in their hands the borrowed revenues of the Government, what

relief could be granted? The Treasury
order, which directed the land-offices to
sell no land but for real money, arrested
the exchange of lands for the .worthless issues of insolvent banks. Deeply sensible
of the sufferings of the community, and too
careful an observer to be ignorant of their
sources, Van Buren adopted the only measure of relief within the power of the Government, by directing a delay in putting
merchants' bonds in suit. But the clamor
of discontent was not hushed by the lenient
interposition. Many were angry because
the specie circular was not suddenly recalled, as if the rescinding of an order now
practically inoperative would have given
solidity to fictitious credits, or would have
arrested the downfall of prices, which the
inevitable laws of trade were effecting in
every part of the cultivated world.

The month of May, 1837, saw the fatal
consummation of the American paper system. The banks in the city of New York

could no longer meet their engagements, and suspended payment of their notes. The same causes produced the same result throughout the country. The deposit banks yielded, in many cases, most eagerly to the example, and, at a time when the national funds were abundant, their faithlessness deprived the Government of the use of its revenues. The people had paid taxes for the support of their institutions, and the parties to whose custody those taxes, after collection, had been intrusted, had placed them beyond their own control and beyond the reach of the Government.

According to existing laws, the universal suspension by the banks of specie payments made it necessary to collect the revenue in gold and silver only. For that end no sudden act of legislation was needed; but the condition of the Treasury demanded that the system of distributing the surplus revenue, by which seven-and-twenty millions of dollars had already been deposited with the

States, should be arrested before the first day of October, when a fourth instalment of nine millions was to be paid. The President, under the pressure of necessity, reluctantly resolved to call an extra session of Congress in September.

The months that intervened were a period of passionate excitement in one part of the community, of earnest reflection in another. Public bodies addressed the President; sincere friends in the various parts of the Union gave him the most opposite advice. The opinion of the party in power had not yet formed itself, and timid advisers, taking advantage of the public irresolution, urged on Van Buren a relaxation of his political system, promising to concessions unbounded popularity. He could only reply by repeating his adhesion to the policy which his whole public life had sustained, which his election had pledged him to uphold, and which every event since his inauguration had but riveted in his convictions.

The President had been, as it were, a pupil of the public mind, educated in the great
school of the nation, a practical statesman,
desirous always of being guided by the
lights of experience.   But now public opinion was silent; it had not yet solved the
mystery of the disease, nor formed its theory of a remedy.   So suddenly had the crisis come, so appalling was its nature, and
so difficult its treatment, that the whole
country hung in suspense, watching what
remedy the calm sagacity of the President
would devise.

Van Buren saw the elements of strife
multiplying about him, and he met the
storm at its height.   Rejecting every nar-
row measure of present expediency, he took
principle for his guide and pushed out boldly upon the deep.   He saw that the Government must occupy a new position.   He saw
that for the moment his party might be
doomed to find itself in a minority.   He
saw that he himself might, perhaps, for a

time, forfeit public favor. He resolved to
meet the crisis in all its difficulties. " We
cannot know how the immediate convulsion
may result for us," he observed to a near
friend, as he was planning his communication to Congress at the extra session ; " but
the people will at all events come right,
and posterity will do me justice. Be the
present issue for good or evil, it is for posterity that I will write this message." And,
anxious to rest the cause of Democracy on
measures and principles which would make
its expected defeat but a transient one, he
recommended to Congress a system which
not one public man in America had ever
before ventured to propose.

The system was a strict recurrence to the
principles of the Constitution and to the
general laws that regulate commerce. ·He
advised to collect only revenue enough for
the wants of the Government ; to collect
that revenue not in uncertain promises, but
in real money, and to keep such revenue

under public responsibilities for public purposes.

How deeply seated must have been the
disease, when such remedies were esteemed
extreme! How entirely had the moneyed
interest allowed itself to be guided by a perverse influence, when a proposition to place
our republic above dependence on banks
and bankers seemed the most daring act of
financial legislation ever recommended in
our country!

The message of the President to the
Twenty-fifth Congress, at its first session,
in September, 1837, is written with vigor
and sound philosophy, having nothing to
be spared, nothing to be modified; its teach-
ings so wisely stated that they cannot be
misconstrued, so ably reasoned that they
carry conviction; being the harmonious and
consistent result of a long career of public
service.

All Americans who connected their ambition with the old European restrictive and

financial systems heard in the message the knell of that system. If the country could, in its finances, follow sound general principle, and avoid interfering with commercial pursuits, class legislation must come to an end. The moneyed interest had compelled the Government to be its servant, to loan to them its revenue, to connect itself with commercial exchanges. The principle of independence would separate the Government from the hierarchy of moneyed institutions, and arrest, at its source, the baneful influence of monopoly.

On the other hand, a new era was opening. The legislation of our country, which is the chief representation of the democracy of the world, had grown out of British legislation after its aristocratic revolution of 1688; and our statute - books showed the anomaly of democratic freedom and laws imitated from the codes of European aristocracies. The message to Congress in its extra session excited a hope that America

was now to enter on a course of legislation
as pure as her principles, to escape from the
control or the bias of interests which had
connected her with the restrictive system.
They saw in the proposed plans something
more than a provision for a temporary and
transient inconvenience. They saw a system wisely founded on enduring principles.

The Government was to separate itself
from the business of the country. It was
no more to attempt the impossible scheme
of controlling seven or eight hundred banks,
chartered by six-and-twenty separate sov-
ereignties; it was no more to disturb exchanges by pretending to regulate them;
and, if it did this, there was hope that the
same wisdom would frown on favoritism of
every kind, would more and more simplify
the operations of the Government, and lead
it to abandon the illiberal purpose of controlling industry by legislative interference.
It was cheering to see that message kin-
dling hope, suppressing rivalries, eradicat-

ing feuds, bringing together men whose
friendships had too long been severed;
winning to its support the energy and com-
pact logic of Calhoun, the integrity and
manly consistency of Brown of North Carolina, of Roane of Virginia, of Niles of Connecticut, and so many others; the massive
strength of Benton, the persuasive prudence
of Buchanan. And it called forth voices of
applause from private life; from Jefferson's
grandson, the pure-minded Randolph; from
men whose voices had long been silent;
from Tazewell of Virginia, and the independent, eloquent McDuffie. Alas! that
any should have wavered and stepped aside
as the party in power entered upon the
strict path of duty.

In the general gloom, it was with calm
intrepidity that the measure was discussed;
and the Senate of the United States became the scene of debates hardly surpassed
in any former deliberate assembly.

At the extra session one important meas-

14

ure was achieved. The process of distribution of the nation's surplus revenue among
the States was checked. To relieve the
community, time was granted to the deposit banks to pay their dues to the public;
and to the merchants who had given bonds
at the custom-house for duties, an extension of their bonds. But the great measure
which Van Buren recommended, though approved by the Senate, could not win for itself a majority in the House.

As yet Van Buren appeared as the stand-
ard-bearer, who had gone in advance of the
army, and summoned the country to move
forward and sustain him. As yet he was
not sustained, and severer trials awaited
him. At the autumn elections Van Buren
was in a minority in the State of New York.

The winter session of 1837 approached.
Unappalled, Van Buren met the crisis. In
the defeats of the autumn he saw only a
means to measure the extent of the disease,
not an interpreter of the rightful remedy.

The people had uttered no oracles; the seven hundred banks, the business classes, roused to spasmodic effort, succeeded where it was not usual; but the facts and principles remained unchanged, and Van Buren persevered in recommending an entire separation of the national treasury from the banks, while the opposition was much inspirited, and with passionate vigor persisted in a desperate fight, with the confident expectation of victory.

The bill for the independent treasury was introduced, but by a combination of conservatives with the anti-democratic opposition, the essential clause that the revenue should be collected in specie could not be carried.

Flushed by appearances that seemed to promise a triumph, and eager in the pursuit of an advantage, Henry Clay, Senator from Kentucky, presented a resolution, which, at his own instance, on the 2d of May, 1838, was read a second time. The resolution directed:

" That no discrimination shall be made as to the currency or medium of payment in the several branches of the public revenue, or in debts or dues to the Government; and that, until otherwise ordered by Congress, the notes of sound banks which are payable and paid on demand in the legal currency of the United States, under suitable restrictions to be forthwith prescribed and promulgated by the Secretary of the Treasury, shall be received in payment of the revenue and of debts and dues to the Government, and shall be subsequently disbursed, in course of public expenditure, to all public creditors who are willing to receive them."

At once, Silas Wright, of New York, a statesman and a friend ever to be relied upon, of an unpretending modesty surpassed only by his merit, moved the reference of the resolution to the Committee on Finance, of which he was the chairman.

Henry Clay answered: " The resolution, or some measure like it, is not only called for by the situation of the country, but its adoption would be attended by the most practical benefits. It contains two principles—first, to do away with all discrimination in the payment of the revenue, whether derived from lands or the customs; and as on that subject the Senate has already expressed its opinion by an almost unanimous vote, I cannot see the necessity of a reference to it. The second provision is, that, until otherwise ordered by Congress, the notes of sound and specie-paying banks shall be received and paid out in the receipts and expenditures of the Government. Now, that principle appears to me so simple that every senator can comprehend it, and therefore there is no necessity for referring it. I am only anxious for a speedy action on the subject." *

"How far is it designed," said Silas Wright, "by this resolution to repeal all former legislation without saying so in terms, I do not know; but an inquiry to see

how far the resolution conflicts with existing laws is highly necessary. In proposing
the reference, I do not wish to delay the action of the Senate on the resolution."

Still Clay denied the propriety of the reference, and argued for the expediency of
passing the resolution. "Now," said he, "is
the accepted time to act." He promised
great benefits to New York from the measure, and concluded by expressing the opinion that nothing but the establishment of a
national bank would effectually remedy the
evils of a disordered currency.

"A reunion with the banks, as proposed
by the resolution," said John C. Calhoun, of
South Carolina, "would at no distant day
be followed by another shock still more ter-
rific than that of May last. . . . A national
bank is out of the question; and if it were
not, would prove one of the greatest calam-
ities that could befall the country."

"What is this resolution?" cried Thomas
H. Benton, of Missouri. "It is a paper-

money and shinplaster resolution, the adoption of which would fill the Treasury with notes which could never be redeemed. . . . I warn the country of the impending mischief. . . . The only way to save the banks is to hold them down to specie payments. . . . The resolution is such a proposition as ought to be discussed, and will be discussed. It is a proposition to fix the attention of a continent. It goes to fundamental principles, and presents the fairest occasion for the array of parties which has yet been seen in Congress. It is paper-money and bank government to the backbone. I am for bringing on the debate with all due speed."

Henry Clay, rising to reply to a remark from the Senator from South Carolina, added: " I am for a Bank of the United States, and wish it so pronounced and so understood that every man, woman, and child should know it."

" There are but two measures," rejoined Calhoun, "that can possibly prevent the rep-

etition of the explosion which it is now contended on all sides must follow, without the
application of some effectual remedy—a
complete and an entire divorce from the
whole system of banks, or the establishment
of a national bank; and of the two, I consider the former as by far the most safe and
effectual."

It was referred to the Committee on Finance; and on the sixteenth day of May, Silas
Wright, of New York, submitted a report,
which, for its lucid and accurate statements
presented in the most unpretending manner, won universal admiration, and will be
remembered alike for its intrinsic excellence
and for having achieved one of the most
memorable victories that ever was gained
in the American Senate.

While the subject was still under consideration, on the occasion of presenting a pe-
tition, Henry Clay more fully expressed his
abiding wish to establish a new national
bank. " The capital," he said, enumerating

its objects, "should not be extravagantly large; I suppose that about fifty millions would answer. The constitutional power ought no longer to be regarded as an open question. There ought to be some bounds to human controversy." And appealing from the actual Congress and the administration, he proposed to make up an issue for future elections.

"A fifty million bank!" said Benton, in the debate on the whole subject: "it cannot be established now, nor until the Democracy of the Union shall have fought their battles of Chæronea and Pharsalia."

After a very long debate, Clay himself, compelled by the irresistible force of argument in the report of Silas Wright, was obliged to retire from his position; and to avoid a worse defeat, on his own motion, the most exceptional part of his resolution was rejected by a vote of forty-four to one. All that remained of an improper nature was, on motion of the Senator from New York, stricken out by a vote of twenty-eight to nineteen.

The Twenty-fifth Congress came to an end; its successor, the Twenty-sixth, was chosen with the question of the currency before the people. In the room of men who were willing to aid in defeating measures of reform, the House of Representatives in the Twenty-sixth Congress was found to contain a majority of those on whom the country could rely.

Following the urgent advice of the President, they entered on the consideration of the independent treasury. They refused to consider it as an insulated question, but upheld it as a measure including a system of policy. The contest between a Bank of the United States and a total separation from the banks involved the question, whether the industry of the country should be left to its natural development, or subjected to artificial and selfish legislation.

At last, on the fourth day of July, 1840,

Van Buren had the happiness of setting his name to the law which established the independent treasury.

That law was demanded by the principles of the party of strict construction, for without it a national bank, "the pioneer of encroachments," would return.

It separated the Government from all interference with the credit of individuals and the credit of States, and so favored entirely the system which tolerates no restrictions on industry, or interference of the Government with private pursuits. Abolishing privileges, and conferring favors on none, it was the symbol of opposition to monopoly of all kinds.

In harmony with advancing civilization, it broke up the partnership between the Government and the credit system, by which the credit and revenue of the Government had been subjected to the accidents of the business of the country.

It removed the Government from that

foreign influence which the credit system, by means of its wide ramifications, was sure to exercise.

It complied with the Constitution, which nowhere permits a loan of the public revenue.

It gave to no set of banks advantages over the rest, but left them all to the employment of their own resources on a system of the utmost impartiality.

It tended to make the flow of credit steady; not adding, in seasons of ardent speculation, new fuel to the flame by throwing the national revenue into banks of deposit to be loaned out for the gain of the banks; but, by withholding the fatal stimulant, to restrain excesses and consequent exhaustion, and to make the flow of credit steady and equable; like a good mill-stream, which never rages with fury, and never fails even in the heat of summer.

It was faithful to the people, taking from them money only for public purposes, saving

that money undiminished by losses from insolvent banks, and sacredly keeping it to be
used according to the laws for the general
good.

It simplified the action of the Treasury,
and so made its operations plain to the common mind.

By forbidding loans of public money, it
diminished the patronage of the General
Government, which no longer could select
from among eight hundred banks its few
favored ones.

It promoted economy in the public expenditures by relieving the class of borrow-
ers from deposit banks and from a United
States Bank from every temptation to favor
an exorbitant revenue.

It prevented utterly the political union
of stock-jobbers and opulent merchants and
corporations with the Government, and thus
favored the purity and permanency of our
institutions.

It was faithful to the country; it did not

allow the people's revenue to be wrested
from the people's Government, and placed
where at any time, in war or in peace, the
use of it for public wants would not be exposed to obstruction from the indiscretions,
the necessities, or the malevolence of banks
of deposit.

It benefited the credit system by holding
over it the gentlest and most certain, the
least oppressive and ever-active, ever-efficient
check.

It gave stability to contracts by main-
taining the standard of value unimpaired
in every part of the Union, preserving as
the measure of value those precious metals
which, being the product of industry, are
themselves of intrinsic value, and thus, without professing to regulate exchanges, it
equalized them throughout the Union.

It gave to manufactures proper protection
by demanding revenue to be paid promptly
on importation, and in specie, and by refusing to make the revenue serve, by means of

loans, as a capital for new importations; at the same time it emancipated the question of the tariff from the influence of deposit banks, which might look to exorbitant duties as a source of profit to themselves.

It checked speculation and tended to keep the money market even. In case of too heavy importations, it gently admonished importers by a tendency to scarcity. The paper system, by its elasticity, expands with rising prices and contracts with descending ones; thus stimulating speculation when it needs a check, and increasing the severity of every pressure. The independent treasury checked importations just when they needed a check; and, in case of falling prices, tended to alleviate the money market by the disbursements of Government, continuing under a diminishing revenue from its previous collections.

It gave a treasury truly independent—independent of foreign sway, independent of the fluctuations of business, independent of bankers and corporations, independent of corrupt influences, independent of all but the will of the people as expressed in the Constitution and the laws.

Such was the independent treasury—a system in harmony with American institutions, based on justice, and productive only of good. It was happy for Van Buren that he was permitted first among our statesmen to propose it, and to set his name to the act consummating its establishment.

Nor did this measure engross exclusively the attention of Van Buren. Great Britain encroached on our north-eastern frontier. Congress placed the resources of the country at his disposition to repel the encroachments; and he succeeded, without the effusion of blood, in driving the English to a position which left the ultimate recognition of the American rights in their full extent a necessary consequence of their concessions.

Nor was attention limited to the Northeast. The Cabinet of Van Buren turned

its care to our immense possessions in the
North-west, and in preparing for its occu-
pation the Department of War planned a
line of military communication extending
to the shores of the Pacific ; for they knew
that it was the duty of our republic to light
from its own hearths the fires of republican
freedom in the vast region of the Oregon.
Our system, which reserves to each individual State the right of development according to its capacities, thus insures diversity, and fearlessly extends the federative system over most extensive territory;
for it knows that its principle of local self-
government for States will insure, in the
midst of union, that diversity of character
and pursuit and interest which is essential
to the full development of national character and power.

Our foreign affairs were conducted with
dignity and success. Indemnities exceed-
ing in amount six millions of dollars were
obtained from various nations for injuries

15

to our commerce. With Mexico we became bound more closely by a just and honorable treaty. Texas and Holland paid indemnities; treaties were matured with nations of South America on the west and on the east; Sardinia and Belgium sought our commerce; and at Athens peaceful intercourse was begun with the government that ruled the now united land of Solon and Lycurgus, of Miltiades and Leonidas.

The removal of the Indian tribes, who, according to previous treaties and acts of legislation, were to find new places of abode beyond the Mississippi, was conducted by the General Government with tenderness and humanity; and more than forty thousand of these emigrants found, on their new and most fertile territory, ample provision for their comfort, their pursuit of agriculture, and their civilization and instruction.

The evils of arbitrary power in the navy had multiplied from neglect. They were alleviated and circumscribed; and as far as depended on the President, by an order in March, 1839, the sailor before the mast was protected against the lash, except as a punishment ordered by a court. This wise humanity received at a later day still further development, but not while Van Buren was President.

To save the public lands from speculators and secure them to actual emigrants, Van Buren was the first among our Presidents to recommend a pre-emption law, thus adopting it as the system of the Government.

From Henry Clay, of Kentucky, the proposed measure, in 1838, met with earnest and uncompromising opposition in Congress. The men for whose benefit it was designed he characterized as a lawless rabble of intruders, as a class entitled to no consideration. He ridiculed the idea of the "moral sense" of these "club-law" men, and was in favor of removing them by force from the lands which they assumed to hold without any color of legal or equitable right. The abuses of the system, he said, outweighed the legitimate benefit which it might afford to honest industry.

There were not wanting eloquent members from the West to vindicate the character of the men thus assailed, as being as honest, industrious, hospitable, peaceable, and law-abiding a population as was to be found in any portion of the Union. On this occasion, Webster, differing from Clay, defended the policy of Van Buren.

Merrick, of Maryland, desired to exclude foreigners from the benefit of the bill, and Henry Clay avowed the pleasure with which he should sustain the amendment; but Walker, Benton, and Buchanan protested against it as illiberal in spirit and foreign to the policy of the New World. The amendment was lost; the measure recommended by Van Buren won majorities in Congress, and the prompt signature of the President made it the law of the land.

In May, 1840, the Democracy of the Union came together in convention at Baltimore; twenty-one States were ably represented, and the voice of the convention was given heartily and unanimously for the nomination of Van Buren as the Democratic candidate for the Presidency.

Never before had the country known a struggle at a Presidential election like that which ensued. The party opposed to Van Buren sought to win the vote of the South by a coalition. They repeated the nomination of William Henry Harrison, who in the previous election had been their candidate for the Presidency. He was by birth a Virginian, the son of one of her statesmen who had been most deeply imbued with the political system which rested on the rights of the States. In 1791 he himself had entered public life as an ensign in the army of the United States, in which he rose to the rank of captain. In 1797 he passed from the army into the office of Secretary of the North-west Territory, and afterwards served in the Sixth Congress as its delegate. In 1811, taking the command of a body of volunteers, he attacked and defeated the British and Indians at Tippecanoe. He took part in the war with Great Britain, and after its close he retired from the army, made his residence in Ohio, was elected to the Fourteenth and Fifteenth Congress of the United States, and afterwards, by the anti-Democratic majority in that State, was sent to the Senate of the United States. He served in that body from December 5, 1825, to May, 1828, when he accepted a commission as Minister of the United States to Colombia. Soon after the inauguration of Andrew Jackson, in 1829, he returned from his mission, and living for more than ten years in retirement a little below Cincinnati, on the banks of the Ohio, had already reached the verge of old age. In his civil career he had, by his unassuming moderation, escaped the inconveniences of noto-

riety and bitter strife; and while the manufacturers of New England received from
him satisfactory assurances of his devotedness to their interests, he united in himself
many of the traditions of Virginia and had
never been at variance with its statesmen.

But to make sure of success, it was necessary for the opponents of Van Buren to gain
the votes of Southern States which were
opposed to their mode of interpretation of
the Constitution and their protective system,
and for that purpose they selected John
Tyler, of Virginia. While representing Virginia in the Senate of the United States,
Tyler had fallen into conflict with Andrew
Jackson, the President. Jackson's motto
was, " The Union must be preserved." Tyler was of the class of statesmen who feared
infringement by the General Government
on local self-government, and whose ruling
maxim was the sovereignty of the States.
Hence, Tyler had separated himself from
the standard-bearers of the party which for

the time made Jackson their leader; and as
the candidate of the coalition for the Vice-
presidency, he never during the campaign
renounced his life-long convictions. His
silence was not censured by any of his supporters at the North, for it strengthened
their chances of winning votes in the South;
but Webster, immediately on the nomination
of Harrison as candidate for the Presidency,
denounced it as " a nomination not fit to be
made."

The public mind was at the time excited
alike by the pecuniary distress from which
the country had not fully recovered, and
from the intense interest attached to the
questions at issue before the people. The
one party, in a season of general suffering,
prodigal of unbounded promises and of mis-
representations, appealed to the sentiment
of sympathy and to the desire of change;
the other addressed itself to the sober reason of the people. Men gathered everywhere in crowds to listen to discussions.

The leading doctrines of political economy became subjects of reflection in every village. But it was observable then, as always, that the feelings may be approached more suddenly than the intellect; besides, the speculations which had pervaded the land had, directly or through ties of friendship, spread their influence into almost every household, and a lurking hope remained that the laws of trade themselves would yield to a change of administration. Yet the millions were excited to a degree never before known. Far greater numbers in proportion to population appeared for the Democratic candidate at the polls than ever before; and the hundreds of thousands who took part did so from conviction; and before long the great and ever-increasing majority, applying alike the tests of science and of experience to the questions of revenue, were converted to their principles and adopted their financial policy; but at the time their candidate was defeated.

One thing more was needed to test the character of Van Buren. Would he bear defeat with dignity?

His last annual message is one of the ablest and best-written documents that had been addressed to Congress by an American Chief Magistrate. Faithful to his principles and free from repining, he did his utmost to prepare the way for his successor. The finances, of which he had received the care under circumstances the most adverse, were left in the exactest order and in ample sufficiency. Every act of legislation was concerted in such a manner as to save his successor from any embarrassment.

Retiring from public life, he left behind him a clear exposition of his financial policy as a beacon-light to the nation.

Returning to his native State as a private man, the city of New York, which sustained Van Buren to the last, poured out its tens of thousands to welcome him, and by the sincerity of their approbation made the moment of his retiring a happy era of his life. At Hudson, as the boat stopped, an old man pressed forward eagerly to pay his tribute to the retired President, who in his younger days had rescued his land from the encroachment of large proprietors. At Kinderhook he was met with an affection which ever increased.

After that period Van Buren enjoyed a quiet tour through the country, not unattended with honors. On public topics his opinions were freely given. When the veto power was endangered by a proposed mangling of the Constitution under pretence of amendment, he defended the preservation of that power.

For Ireland, he expressed the unanimous wish of America—that she may recover the inalienably rightful possession of local self-government and legislation.

To a Convention of Indiana he expressed himself freely on the tariff, pleading for the constitutional right of discrimination, yet finding the limit to duties in the needed amount of revenue.

To remedy the evil of official patronage, he proposed for the United States what he had successfully proposed to New York—a transfer of patronage, when possible, from the Central Government to the people.

The characteristics of Van Buren as a statesman were a firm reliance on principle and, in the darkest hour, a bright and invigorating hopefulness.

When thoughtful leaders of his party were appalled, Van Buren knew how to dispel apprehension by his serene presence and addresses. Few statesmen have relied less on patronage, and few public men were ever more free from personal intrigue. This I know from his friends, and have had opportunity to observe.

His course was that of a statesman devoted to principle and studying the lessons of experience. Hence, as a statesman, he was the pupil of the public mind of his time, deciding questions, as they arose, in favor of liberty.

He avowed that the public mind was ever his study. Against it he would never rise in rebellion. If the majority erred, he knew no appeal to arms against its will; but, acknowledging that the works of human hands and the thoughts of human minds are inadequate and imperfect, recognizing no higher earthly tribunal than the common mind of the American people, he admitted of no appeal but from the passions of the present hour to the wisdom of the next, from the enlightened judgment of to-day to the more enlightened "sober second thought" of to-morrow.

Thus far in his career he pursued a system of progressive legislation, not rejecting the past, but, with moderation and avoiding glaring transitions, he sought to improve and reform the past.

This restraining caution and moderation of character his opponents called non-committal, thinking his opinions undecided because he did not share their passions.

The private life of Van Buren was unblemished and unblamed. In youth he opposed the old United States Bank, and its substitute, the Bank of America. With consistency and vigilance he resisted the encroachments of the banking power, and with early and almost solitary sagacity, predicted the evil consequences of the prevailing system of corporate banks. In the Senate of New York and of the United States he led the way in abolishing imprisonment for debt; he opposed the spirit of monopoly in all its forms, and would never become a share-holder in a corporation established by the Legislature of which he was a member. He assisted to overthrow property restrictions on the elective franchise, and to achieve for the people of New York general suffrage. As President, he was the first to recommend grants of pre-emption rights to settlers. By his especial direction, a public ordinance secured to the laborers on public works opportunity for due domestic enjoyment and repose. Those who knew him longest and most intimately used to challenge his most inveterate opponents to point to one instance in his political career of more than thirty years, where the conflict was between the assumptions of the few and the rights of the many, between the pretensions of privilege and the just liberties of the masses, in which he was not found sustaining the latter and battling for human rights.

THE END.